Mr Dickens & Master Betty

Mr Dickens
&
Master Betty

Alan Stockwell

MR DICKENS AND MASTER BETTY

ISBN 978-0-9565013-2-5

Published 2010 by

VESPER HAWK

www.vesperhawk.com

"In childhood, the moments of consciousness that we later recall occur precisely when we are not happy, but these high moments transform themselves by a miracle into a memory of happiness, as though stones had hatched."

Candia McWilliam *Debatable Land*

"Most men begin life with struggles, and have the vanity sufficiently knocked about the head and shoulders to make their kinder fortunes the more welcome. Mr Betty had his sugar first, and his physic afterward. . . . I wish with all my heart we had let him alone."

Leigh Hunt *Autobiography*

MONEY
HISTORICAL NOTE

The currency in use during the period of the story was based on pounds, shillings and pence (*£sd*).

£1 = 20 shillings   1 shilling = 12 pence

These denominations were rendered variously as, for example,

£209	(Two hundred and nine pounds)
£37.10s	(Thirty seven pounds and ten shillings)
£203.14.6 or £203 14s 6d.	(Two hundred and three pounds, fourteen shillings and sixpence)
7/-	(7 shillings)
4/6 or 4/6d	(four shillings and sixpence – colloquially called "four and six")

A guinea was originally a gold coin whose value was fixed in 1717 as £1.1s.0d. Although the coin itself was abolished in 1813 the term guinea survives to the present day and the value in modern UK currency is £1.05.

Part One
1835

Master Betty

FAME may be fleeting, wealth must ebb and flow, but over all is man's craving to be remembered.

Mr William Henry West Betty exudes an aura of complacency and well-being. He is forty-five years of age but drinking and excessive eating coupled with a sedentary mode of life have combined to give him an appearance of at least ten years more. He is corpulent and his face lacks any defining character or feature. This is rather surprising because in his youth he was lauded for his beautiful hair, his graceful figure and his sweet visage. Mr Betty is a rich man but the house in which he sits is comfortable rather than luxurious. On this particular afternoon he is alone in the house as his wife is away for several weeks visiting friends in the country and she has taken her personal maid with her. His son is away at school and his household staff comprises one maid-of-all-work who has been despatched to buy a further supply of Burton-ale.

He shovels a few lumps of sea-coal and throws a log on the fire as he awaits a visitor. He is slightly anxious because he cannot remember his visitor's name. This worries him because he can, if pushed to it, still remember the entire roles of Hamlet, Norval and many other characters.

He hears the door bell jangle. Glancing at the clock he sees his visitor is punctual to the second. Mr Betty appreciates that fact as, in his working life, he had been a slave to schedules and stage-coach time-tables. Just as he lumbers to the door he recalls his visitor's name is Charlie. He opens the door to reveal a very fashionably dressed man who, although young in years, has had the experience of menial labour, been a lawyer's clerk, a shorthand writer at Doctors' Commons and is currently parliamentary correspondent for the *Morning Chronicle*. He is, moreover, an aspiring novelist and his purpose in visiting today is to act as amanuensis to Mr Betty.

— Good day to you, Charlie. Come you in, come you in. Let me take your hat and cane. I apologise for the lack of a servant to open the door. I have despatched her hence on an errand. Sit you down, sir. Draw up to the fire, it is chill outdoors, is it not? Let me pour you a warming drink.

— It's rather early in the day I think, sir.

— Is it? Well perhaps a cordial?

— I would prefer to come straight to the business in hand if we may?

— You found me all right? They do say that if you stop anybody within half a mile of here and ask for Mr Betty they can show you to my door! Hogarth recommended you as a very talented up-and-coming young man. Said you wrote pieces for the newspapers and so on. Yes. Well. I understand you can do this special note-taking?

— I've learned shorthand, yes.

— That's it – shorthand. Well what I want is this – did I explain the other night?

— You said you wanted to write your memoirs and you preferred to relate them to a competent writer so they could be written up professionally.

— That is it. Exactly. You see I do not like these authors who say "I did this" and "Then I did that." It sounds as though they are boasting all the time. Now I am not a boaster. Never have been. I would prefer my story told in the third person. I am not much of a scholar – though I did go to university. I thought it would be a good idea if I related my tale to some clever young fellow like yourself who could take it down. Take it away and work it up into a proper memoir and an interesting read. Do you follow my meaning?

— Yes. I can easily do that for you.

— Good, good. Are you sure you will not partake of something? I could prepare some tea and cakes. My maid has just slipped out but I am sufficiently competent in domestic duties to make tea and I am sure we have a dainty morsel somewhere.

— I'd rather get on with the job in hand if we may, sir.

— Very well. As you wish. Did I suggest any figure to you for the work?

— Twenty-five guineas was mentioned.

— Ah, I said that did I? Right. Yes, that is correct. Is that agreeable?

— Perfectly; although I don't as yet know the amount of work involved.

— Quite right, you do not. What I suggest is that I sit here and relate my story as I recollect it. You take it down with your shorthand. Then you go away and write it up. Send it back to me and I will go through it and make any necessary corrections or alterations. Or add things that I might have forgotten and so on.

— I would then be required to do further work on it?

— Oh, no, no. Once it is written up your job done. I will have the bulk of it there. It will be a simple matter to tidy it up. I can do that. It is the style and manner of the thing that I lack.

— Of course the remuneration will depend on how long the work turns out to be and how much trouble it takes me.

— To be sure. I do not intend a *magnum opus*. Far from it. In fact I want it to be fairly brief so that it can be sold very cheaply.

— I see.

— It is not my whole life I wish to relate. Much of that is as tedious as the next man's. No. But I have an astounding story to tell. Can you believe that? Seeing me here now you cannot believe that I once astonished the world, can you? You are a young man so all I have to tell you happened long before you were born. What I am about to relate centres around the beginning of the century. Do you know any history, Charlie?

— A little. But I would prefer not to be addressed as Charlie.

— What about the year 1805? Can you recall any significant happenings of that year?

— Every schoolboy knows that was the year of the Battle of Trafalgar and the death of Admiral Lord Nelson.

— You are quite right. In that year the entire nation was on tenterhooks expecting the invasion of Buonaparte. Then there was Nelson's great victory. But I banished all thoughts of war from the newspapers. The cream of society could not care a fig for Old Boney. Their only concern was for me!

— You, sir?

— Yes, sir, me, sir! Ah, you find that incredible? The smallest item concerning myself was good for a whole column of newsprint. Ladies of fashion and quality vied with each other to woo me to their homes. The future King of England, our present monarch himself, sent daily to enquire of my welfare. I should think all that surprises you, eh?

— Indeed it does, sir.

— Can you guess why I was the idol of the aristocracy? Do you know why the highest in the land gave me their favours?

— Perhaps you did some heroic deed? You must have been very young. Perhaps you were a midshipman and bravely fought with Nelson?

— Me, a sailor! No, sir. Not at all. I was the Young Roscius!

— Sir?

— You have not heard of Master Betty the Young Roscius?

— I'm afraid not, sir. I know you are Mr Betty.

— Ah, the transience of fame. In my day I was as famous as Napoleon Buonaparte. More crowds came to gaze at me than came to look upon George III. And now I am forgotten. Are you interested in the thespian art at all, Charlie?

— Yes, I'm very keen. In fact I've done a little acting myself.

— Indeed?

— Only as an amateur of course.

— Of course. And what roles have you played?

— So far I've only played one – Fabian in *Twelfth Night*. That's all I could afford.

— Afford? I do not understand.

— Well, sir, you have to pay to play, as the saying is.

— Pay to play? That is surely the wrong way round? When I was an actor they paid me.

— Oh, yes, professional players. The amateur system is different. A private theatre will announce the play and offer the parts to enthusiasts at a price depending on the importance of the role. In the production I took part in Malvolio was two pounds and Orsino thirty shillings. Fabian was only five shillings.

— What an extraordinary idea! I have never heard anything like it.

— It's quite commonplace, sir. So many people like to have a go at acting.

— "Have a go at acting"! My God, if Mrs Siddons were alive today to hear that! But then I do not suppose you have even heard of Mrs Siddons?

— Indeed I have, sir.

— And Garrick? Kemble? Cooke? Kean?

— I do have some knowledge of history, Mr Betty. Some of those names are known to me. I once saw Edmund Kean myself, shortly before he died.

— Did you indeed? I must not be too severe. After all I cannot expect you to know about people who died before you were born. May I ask how old you are, Charlie?

— Twenty-four, sir. I was born in the year 1812. And I would prefer you did not call me Charlie.

— 1812. Ah, well, there we have it. That was the year that Cooke died and Mrs Siddons retired. We do not have actors like that today.

— We have the great Macready.

1831

Charles's days were spent in drudgery and boredom taking down the law in action at Doctors' Commons, only relieved by nights of gaiety and fun at the theatre where he, like many of his generation, was a passionate admirer of the eminent actor William Charles Macready. Whenever the great man appeared in a new role Charles was one of the first in the queue to witness it. But not only was Charles a devotee of the theatre, he was desirous of being a part of it. He revelled in amateur dramatics with his pals. Charles was leading the sort of life many young men followed – accepting the necessity of dull, boring work during the day to give themselves the means to enjoy their leisure time. Many young men grew old doing nothing more than this until they realised that not only was their work irksome but soon they would be unable to do it at all. An old man trying to live his life in the manner of a young man is a sorry sight, especially when his financial means are limited. Fortunately a benevolent God creates young men with an interest in young women. A respectable young man soon comes to realise that respectable young women are, in turn, interested in him. But most young ladies seek a future with a man who will make something of himself and it is not unusual that, if the young man is personable enough, his future father-in-law will enhance his climb up the ladder of ambition. There is also a freedom and camaraderie amongst young fellows that enables them to make practical use of the friendships and acquaintances they acquire socially.

Charles considered himself one of the smartest nineteen-year-olds in London. He made a point of dressing in a fashionable manner and knew that he often turned heads when he walked along the street. At the moment he followed fashion but he would much prefer to be in a position to lead it. It was all very well having a career as a parliamentary reporter but that was seasonal. When Parliament was in recess he was out of work. A career must have more stability. He could not even contemplate marriage unless he had a more settled way of life. He still wondered if there was an opening in the law. Although he had thrown up the drudgery of a law clerk he had progressed, through his own diligence, to become a shorthand writer at Doctors' Commons. He had faith in his abilities but was at a loss to know how to channel them. Should he become a famous barrister? A writer? Or perhaps an actor?

He had acted in plays with his friends and was considered to be a good amateur player. Everybody praised his imitations of the famous and the everyday. He decided that the stage would have the benefit of his talents. He wrote to Mr Bartley the stage manager at Covent Garden theatre and asked for an audition. He admitted to his professional inexperience but stressed his outstanding ability to mimic in his own person the voice, traits and peculiarities that he observed in others. What he did not say was that he was a great admirer of the current star comedian Mr Charles Matthews whose trademark speciality was copying the voice, traits and peculiarities he observed in others. Mr Bartley replied civilly, offering him an audition date when he would be heard by Mr Charles Kemble the theatre manager.

Persuading his sister Fanny to accompany him on the piano he got up an audition piece comprising his best imitations which they then rehearsed thoroughly. Whatever Charles undertook, whether it be wrapping blacking-pots, copying legal documents, accurately taking and transcribing debates or merely acting on the stage, his aim was to be the best of all the people doing that particular thing.

The night before the audition Charles went to bed full of confidence in his carefully prepared and thoroughly rehearsed audition piece. Fanny had been quite unable to play on occasion because she was so amused by her brother's antics. However, when the day of the audition dawned he awoke with a streaming cold and knew he could not possibly give of his best. He was obliged to send a message to Fanny and a note to Mr Bartley excusing himself with profuse apologies and stating he would re-apply for a new audition date during the following year. He never did re-apply as he channelled all his spare time into writing but he continued to love the theatre, and amateur dramatics, and idolised William Charles Macready.

— Macready! I know him well of old. He is too concerned with being respectable. Too conscious of his position as head of the profession. Safe but stolid is William. You should have seen Cooke! George Frederick Cooke; there was an actor! I worked with him many a time. He supported me in *Douglas*. He was Lord Glenalvon, the villain of the piece. He was excellent at villains. Richard III was his star part. He went to America and died there. The year you were born, Lord love us! Cooke was a great player but an unreliable man. Forever having to step forward and apologise for his old complaint.

— What was that?

— Drink. Now, me – you could always rely on William Betty both as a boy and a man. I took my duty to the public very seriously. But to business! I want you to set down my story.

— Very well, sir, I'll do that. I've come equipped although I would ask that I may interrupt your flow to clarify any point that seems unclear.

— Oh, that is understood. I shall not deliver a lecture to you. I hope we shall be having a friendly chat. I have made a few notes here that I shall need to refer to from time to time. Dates and that sort of thing.

— Right. Then please commence.

— I was born on the 13th September 1791. That makes me forty-five years of age. I was born at Shrewsbury in the county of Shropshire. My mother's family was called Stanton. Stantons had held the manor of Hopton Wafers for centuries.

— Pardon me! Wafers, was it?

— Yes. Hopton. W – A – F – E – R – S. May I proceed? We lived at a house called Hopton Court. My father was an Irishman. He was the eldest son of an eminent physician, Dr Betty of Lisburn. I was christened William Henry West Betty. I lived at Hopton Court until I was five. Then we went to Ireland where my father had an estate. A beautiful seat called Mill Hill near Lisburn. My father was in business. Linen manufacture near

Ballynahinch. B – A – L – L – Y – N – A – H – I – N – C – H. One day my father declaimed

> I'll therefore buy some cottage near his manor,
> Which done, I'll make my men break ope his fences;
> Ride o'er his standing corn, and in the night
> Set fire on his barns; or break his cattle's legs.

That's Sir Giles Overreach in *A New Way to Pay Old Debts*. Of course I did not know that at the time. My father simply told me it was called acting. I think here, Charlie, you could put something like "What great events spring from occasions apparently trivial." It was from that day my destiny was determined.

— How old were you then?

— What? Oh, I would be only eight or nine years old. I took a great interest in this special way of speaking called acting. I learned speeches from plays and recited them to my mother's friends. My mother was very pleased to see this interest. The local speech was very uncouth. She did not want me, an English gentleman, lapsing into that base mangling of the English tongue.

1801

It was Saturday afternoon and William wanted to be out with the other boys. His mother strongly disapproved of the local children. They were thoroughly Irish and many were the offspring of workers at the flax mill. Even the respectable boys from good Irish families spoke with that deplorable accent. She did not want her William to pick up such depraved speech. He was an English gentleman, even if his father was Irish. Her family had been country gentry in the heart of England for a thousand years. She was not going to have her precious boy turned into a hooligan.

"You are not to go into the village, William. I do not want you mixing with uncouth boys."

"No, Mama."

"It's no good saying 'No, Mama' in that resigned way. I want you to heed what I say."

It was bad enough during the week when he had to do lessons with his tutor but this was Saturday. The mill had closed until Monday and all workers, except those on farms who still had animals to tend on a Sunday, were at leisure until then. Even the few boys who went to school were allowed Saturday afternoon off. Saturday afternoon was the highlight of William's week. Nothing other than Church happened on a Sunday as the local priest ruled with an iron rod and nobody in the vicinity dared to do anything on a Sunday without his permission. Even the English people in the town were obliged to be circumspect in their activities on a Sunday.

William approached his friends cautiously. He never really knew how they would greet him. Some days they were dismissive and quite rude. Sometimes they mocked him. But on other occasions he was greeted with warmth and friendliness and allowed to join in with whatever mischief the lads were getting up to.

"Hello there, Angle, come and help with this!" called Micky. The Irish boys had taken to calling William by the nickname of Angle because one day the priest had told the story of Pope Gregory seeing blond blue-eyed boys for sale as slaves in the market place of Rome. When the Pope asked who they were he was told they were Angles who had been captured from a far off land called Britannia. Gregory had replied "Not Angles but Angels." One of the lads had obviously been impressed with this tale and, because William hailed from England, had immediately called him Angle. William was relieved – at least it was not Angel and a decided improvement on Girlie, this being the first nickname they had bestowed upon him on account of his tumbling mass of wavy hair of which his mother was so proud.

"What are you doing?"

"We're damming the stream to make a pool," answered Micky.

"We're going swimming," added another boy.

The group of boys set about willingly, in an organised fashion, to stem the flow of the stream so that a pool would build up in the bend of the river where it was at its widest. In winter the rains fell heavily and the stream became a fast flowing river. Indeed it was the very water that fed William's father's flax mill, the machinery being worked by the flow. But in a dry summer such as the present one the flow was sluggish and the level low. The boys always thought that God had not ordained things properly – when the weather was cold and horrid the water was deep enough to swim in, but when summer brought hot sunny weather and a welcome dip highly sought after, the stream was feeble and shallow.

Eventually the dam was created and the water began deepening. The boys shed their clothes and leapt and splashed about with great merriment.

"T'will be even better tomorrow, when the water gets

deeper," said Micky.

"We won't be able to come on a Sunday," said Murph.

"Who won't?" challenged Micky. "You just see. I haven't gone to all this trouble just for one afternoon."

Mickey was less obedient to the priest and local society than his chums and, although not one of them responded to his boast, they all secretly knew that if Micky were there the following day he would be there on his own.

The time passed in great jollity and none of the boys got too carried away with the horseplay. As the sun started dipping behind the mountains they realised that they had better come out and try and dry off before making their way homewards. Abandoning the pool they raced each other up and down the field to get dry before donning the assortment of rags they called clothing.

William returned home happy and content. It was a rare occasion that he was able to spend time doing boyish things in the company of other boys. He knew he would be in trouble when he got home because he was filthy and his clothes were wet. The boys may have made a swimming pool but they could not swim and had spent the hours leaping and cavorting and churning up all the silt and mud that had been dormant on the river bed.

However, the scolding William got on Saturday evening was nothing to the row that erupted on Monday morning when William's father discovered the water supply to drive his flax mill had ceased completely. This was a serious matter and livelihoods were at stake. When the dam was found and the makeshift wall broken through, the search commenced for the culprits. Of course William knew who the culprits were, as after all, he was one of them. But his parents had no idea how much he had ingratiated himself into the boys' gang and never dreamed, after William's first denial, that he would actually know all about it. Although not yet realising it, William had started to acquire the basic art of an actor. He was able to convincingly pretend.

— There were a few English people in our locality but none had children with them. Those with families preferred that their children were sent to school in England. My mother's social circle was, perforce, inclusive of the better class Irish people. Well, one day my father took me into Belfast to see the great actress Mrs Siddons. You said you knew Mrs Siddons's name? She was the greatest player of her day. Belfast was honoured by the visit of this great lady. Between you and me, Charlie, most actresses have quite lax principles, some are little better than prostitutes, but Mrs Siddons was renowned for her personal dignity and moral authority. She was respected by all. Do you know, Lord Byron once said he would as soon as think of going to bed with the Archbishop of Canterbury as he would Mrs Siddons?

— Her name and reputation are well-known to me.

— I had never been in a theatre before – Mother would not normally permit it. But Mrs Siddons was respectable. When I saw Mrs Siddons acting Elvira – the play was Sheridan's tragedy *Pizarro* – I was overwhelmed. I think Elvira was her finest role. She portrayed an Inca female thirsting for revenge after betrayal by her lover Pizarro. She prevails upon a follower called Rolla to kill Pizarro then, overcome by guilt and remorse, she retreats to a convent. Very strong.

1802

William's father had secured a box for one of the performances. William's mother was not pleased. She was a religious woman and regarded the theatre to be the work of the devil and the players who strutted there destined for damnation. Even Mrs Siddons's moral rectitude would not sway her. She declared nothing would induce her to go. She did not want William to go either. She did not want her son tainted by association with such a wicked thing as the stage.

"Of course the boy shall go. It is a wonderful opportunity for him to see great acting. Why do you object so? You do not mind him standing on a stool and reciting in our drawing-room to your gaggle of friends."

"That's different, as well you know."

"It is so. Very different. That is mere reciting – at the theatre we shall see real acting as it should be done."

As was usual, William's father was obeyed and the trip to Belfast was organised. William's mother declined to be of the party so a coach bearing William, his father and two respectable neighbours who were close associates of his father set off for Belfast. William could hardly contain his excitement. He had never been in a theatre before and did not know what to expect.

He was overwhelmed. The whole evening was as magic. Firstly the candle-lit theatre with its benches packed with hundreds of people, then the music from the orchestra set on the floor in front of the stage, but greatest of wonders when the green baize curtain rose – a whole new different world. No longer were the people in Belfast. They were in a far away country called Peru and, not only that, they were in a distant time. He was watching Spanish soldiers invading the Inca people. And they were not just still pictures like he had seen at lectures; they were real actual people speaking to him – telling him what they had done, were doing, were going to do. Fighting each other, killing each other, and loving each other. It was wonderful.

Every so often in the course of the evening there was a break and William was in stunned raptures waiting for the drama to go on again, for ever and ever. "'Tis only in sport," said his father, "they do not harm one another. It is called acting. It is all pretence."

Of course it had to end and it ended with the people shouting and clamouring for Mrs Siddons. The green baize curtain had fallen but that famous lady walked out in front of it and curtseyed solemnly to her public. Some people threw flowers on to the stage. The people up in the top of the theatre, which William's father said was called the gallery, stamped their feet and set up such a din that the very fabric of the building was in danger. Mrs Siddons, with a final grand gesture that embraced her public, the theatre, indeed the entire world, then left the stage for the last time and it was all over.

Although it had seemed a long journey getting to the theatre, the journey home passed in a twinkling and it appeared no time before the neighbours were dropped off at their house and the carriage arrived home. William's mother had waited up.

"If I cannot be a player when I grow up I shall die!" declared William.

William's father laughed heartily and his mother burst into tears.

— I regret I don't know the play *Pizarro,* Mr Betty.

— No. Not done much nowadays. Well, I realised now what acting was all about. I returned home as in a dream. I told my parents that I should die if I could not be a player. I could think of nothing but the divine Elvira and learned all her speeches "O man! ye who, wearied by the fond fidelity of virtuous love, seek in the wanton's flattery a new delight." Great stuff! I became obsessed with the art of acting. My father took me to see Mr Atkins, the manager of the theatre.

— At Belfast?

— Yes. I recited for him. He was a man of a most friendly disposition and agreed with my father about my extraordinary abilities. He said he had never dared hope to see another Garrick but that he saw one in Master Betty. That was encouraging was it not? David Garrick was the greatest actor of all time. So we come now to my debut on any stage anywhere. 16th August 1803. That is the date. It was announced that a young gentleman only eleven years old, whose theatrical abilities have been the wonder and admiration of all, would enact the role of Osman in *Zara.*

— What was the reason for choosing that play as your debut?

— What? I have no idea. Mr Atkins engaged me for four nights and I was to do a different play each night. I had got up Osman, Young Norval in *Douglas,* Rolla in *Pizarro* – I could hardly play Elvira! – and Romeo. I am not sure how the decision was made upon the plays. That was never in my command. My Friends always arranged with the manager and I was told which role I was to play.

— Your Friends?

— My father and – other advisers.

— I see. Your debut?

— I caused a total furore. The whole town was talking about my perform-ance. The *Belfast News Letter* said "The Young Gentleman's person is handsome, his deportment majestic, his voice bold and melodious and was truly astonishing. He bids fair to rival the first tragedians of the stage and may justly be styled the Minor Roscius." Make a note, Charlie. My first-ever review. See, I have an album of newspaper cuttings that you may take away with you and use for quotations. I played to full houses and much acclaim. My fame spread and I was engaged to play at Dublin. I was such a success I added Hamlet. I got that up in three mornings.

— Three mornings? That seems a brief time to learn such a long and complicated part?

— But I was a Gift from God. I had only to learn the words. Most actors have to study their roles and rehearse them. I was a Child of Nature. All that came to me naturally. My talents were God-given, not acquired by study. I was inspired by God in the same way as the musical prodigy Mozart.

— You compare yourself to Mozart?

— He produced the sounds of Heaven with his keyboard. I gave utterance from my throat. Ah, yes. Dublin. The house there held four hundred pounds a night. We did very well. The terms were that we had a share of the house. Then on to Cork and all the major towns of Ireland. There was wild enthusiasm for me everywhere. Then my father had an offer from Mr Jackson the manager of the theatres in Edinburgh and Glasgow. The offer was for fourteen performances in Glasgow with an option for a similar engagement to follow in Edinburgh if I made a success. After I had made my debut for him – Young Norval in *Douglas* – Mr Jackson placed in print that I was received with the greatest bursts of applause he could ever remember from any audience. "No words can express the full extent of his surprising endowments. We had all thought the school of Garrick was dead; but no more – here it was revived. All Young Roscius' words and gestures are true to character and passion." I was always called Master Betty the Young Roscius. Roscius was the most famous actor of ancient times.

— So I believe.

MAY 1804

After the first night at Glasgow Mr Jackson asked Mr Betty to bring his son to see him during the morning.

"Now young fellow, tell me all about yourself. I want to write a book about you. Tell me how you became an actor. You are a veritable prodigy; do you know what that means? It means somebody who does something prodigious. That is to say something astonishing. You are a prodigy because you are only a boy yet you are able to act better than famous adult actors. I have seen them all. I saw David Garrick play and you are his equal. You have heard of Mr Garrick, I take it?"

"Yes, sir. He was the greatest actor who ever lived."

"In fact I may make so bold as to declare that in many respects you surpass him. Now I shall write a book all about you and it shall be on sale at the theatre. It will sell like hot cakes. Why are you laughing, boy?"

"Books like hot cakes, that's very funny, sir."

Mr Jackson looked blank then, realising that this must be the first time the lad had ever heard this commonplace expression, saw how droll the idea was and laughed too. "I suppose it is!" And the two laughed companionably as Mr Jackson explained that it meant the book would sell thousands of copies and make a lot of money.

"You, young sir, are going to be very famous and you will make a great deal of money. I hope when you are a big star in London you will remember all we lesser mortals who helped you on your way. I have no doubt that many writers will want to interview you and write about you but I aim to get in first. I shall arrange that copies of the book be on sale at all the theatres where you appear. I am going to write your life story although you have not yet lived many years. I shall tell of your early life in Ireland and how you first discovered your incredible talent when reciting for your mother's friends. Then I shall detail your early triumphs and enumerate the parts you have played and so on.

And of course I shall quote extensively from all the wonderful newspaper reviews you have already garnered. Now be a good boy and answer my questions and we will soon get through this."

Then, as Mr Hough had suggested, Mr Jackson started his questioning in preparation for his book.

— Mr Jackson actually wrote a book about me and sold it at the theatre in Edinburgh where I proceeded next. There, though at that time I would not have believed it possible, my reception was even more rapturous. Here you could say something like "However, it was a mere zephyr compared to the storm our hero was soon to raise on his debut in London." I think that has a goodly turn of phrase. Have you got that?

— Mere zephyr compared to storm.

— Mr Home the author of *Douglas* came to see me play there. He was very old by then. He said he had never seen Young Norval played better in all his life. I portrayed the part exactly as he had imagined him. Lord Meadowbank, the most prominent aristocrat in Edinburgh, condescended to interest himself in my welfare.

JULY 1804

Lord Meadowbank was very taken with Master Betty and attended all his performances, leading the applause from his prominent box. He made the acquaintance of Mr and Master Betty and was a regular visitor both backstage and at their hotel.

"I hope you are not neglecting your son's education, Mr Betty. He is obviously an intelligent boy and his brain should be constantly kept alert with absorbing new matters of all description. I have brought you some books which I, myself, have recently read with great interest and pleasure. I think they will stimulate your son's mind, give him food for thought and introduce him to a wider world than that of the theatre. They are all recent publications so I urge you to treasure them during your stay. You may return them to me before your departure."

"You are very kind, my lord," replied Mr Betty, "I thank you on behalf of my son who is still sleeping off the fatigues of last night's exertions." He made a low bow as Lord Meadowbank nodded and swept out to his waiting carriage.

Mr Betty looked at the books that had been left: *Minstrelsy of the Scottish Border, Life of Geoffrey Chaucer the Early English Poet* and *Observations on the Theory and Practice of Landscape Gardening,* and knowing what response they would get if he proffered them to his son, put them in the bottom drawer of the chest and made a note to remind himself to return them before leaving the city.

All the gentry of the town competed to take Young Roscius out for carriage drives. The gentlemen of Edinburgh tend to be of a serious disposition. They are much given to disputation of scientific subjects and medical matters, but they also take a real interest in the theatre and will dispute the merits of plays and players just as earnestly. As the capital of Scotland, Edinburgh has its own thriving culture that is in no way inferior to London and numbers many eminent writers, scientists and inventors among its population.

As Lord and Lady Meadowbank rattled along in their carriage with Mr and Master Betty sitting opposite, the noble lord was holding forth on his favourite topic – the education of the young.

"All children should learn to read. And I do mean all, Mr Betty; not just boys but girls too. And not just the upper classes but *all* children, even the children of the working class and the poor. Reading is a gateway to a better life. It stimulates the imagination, it shows the poor that there are things to strive for and not to – "

"Oh, haud yer wheesht, Allan," said Lady Meadowbank. "You know as well as I do that if you educate the lower classes they will learn to be dissatisfied with their lot and rise up in revolt like the French. Do you want that? We would be the first to have our heads chopped off, we leading aristocrats."

Mr Betty, who believed in cultivating the upper classes on the grounds that their support meant increased business at the theatre, did not wish a domestic spat to arise and be associated with Young Roscius, and so attempted to head off further disputation.

"It was very kind of you to give William *The Minstrel.* I am sure we will both read it with pleasure and it will be forever a remembrance of your extreme kindness during our stay here in Edinburgh."

"It is the most valuable creation by the most eminent person bearing your name, Mr Betty. That is why I thought it would be of great interest to your son."

"I really do not know why you say that, Allan. The book is by somebody called James Beattie – a different name from Betty entirely."

"It is not a different name, my dear, you are mistaken. Beattie is the Scottish manner of spelling and pronouncing the same name."

Lady Meadowbank knew it was fruitless to argue about such things and she returned to trying to interest and entertain the boy who was lethargically slumped in the corner opposite. She thought he really was an insipid child who seemed to take no interest in the various wonders she pointed out. "Look, William, that great hill is called Arthur's Seat because King Arthur is supposed to have set his throne on the summit. It is, in fact, an extinct volcano."

William raised a bleary eye and peered upwards. "An extremely high hill so near to the city, my lady," he said and lapsed into silence again as he contemplated the forthcoming evening and tried to remember which part Mr Hough had said he was to play.

When the time came for the Bettys to move on, Lord Meadowbank sent a letter listing recommended volumes he thought Master Betty could read with profit and, as a farewell gift, a copy of *The Expedition of Humphrey Clinker* an old favourite of his that he was sure would amuse William as it treated of comical journeys and it would be a comfort on his travels.

— We had a very exciting time in Edinburgh what with carriage drives and card parties. My father loved cards and was always ready for a wager. My mother was great with child and had come over from Ireland to join us. However, on learning the itinerary planned for me, she realised that it would be foolish for her to travel with us in her condition so it was arranged that she would remain in Edinburgh until after the baby was born. Edinburgh is probably the finest place to be if you have medical matters as the population there is full of doctors and surgeons and all sorts of scientific people.

Well that was Edinburgh. You can abstract further information from the cuttings. Now we were to go to Birmingham where the manager was Mr M'Cready.

— Macready?

AUGUST 1804

William M'Cready was the manager of the New Street Theatre in Birmingham. It was his proud boast that it cost more to build than any other theatre in the provinces and the gallery was the largest and best in Europe. It was certainly large for a provincial theatre, seating some two thousand people. The elegant façade, built only twenty years previously, was recognised as unparalleled throughout the country. Master Betty and his Friends arrived tired and weary after a long and tedious journey from Edinburgh. It had taken them four days. The coach had gone into a ditch and broken a wheel near Ripon and a horse had cast a shoe and gone lame at Belper. The overnight inn at Catterick had been riddled with bugs and William had been sick all through the Peak District.

Mr M'Cready the manager at Birmingham had engaged Master Betty for thirteen nights at ten pounds a night through Mr Jackson, relying entirely on that gentleman's recommendation. When he saw the thin, tired, frail boy he was very doubtful of his deal.

"Mr Betty, I am not sure your boy is capable of carrying out the contract as agreed. He seems very, er, untheatrical. Does he have the ability to carry a play?"

"Master Betty has been acclaimed throughout Ireland and in the two principal theatres in Scotland. I offered his services to you, sir, because I thought you were one of the leading theatres in England. I wanted you to have the opportunity of staging Master Betty's English debut."

"Well I value that, Mr Betty, but England is not Ireland or Scotland; the audiences tend to be more sophisticated. I do not denigrate the Irish or the Scottish people when I say that, sir. I am Irish myself and it is well-known that all the leading players and playwrights in the English theatre hail from Ireland. But I am running a business here, Mr Betty, I cannot afford to take risks and I am bound to say, having seen your boy, he does not strike me as likely to be the outstanding attraction you claimed in our correspondence."

"Very well, sir, if you wish to break your legal contract with us I am at liberty to sue you for breach. But that will not be necessary. Master Betty is in great demand at theatres all over this land and I can swiftly arrange an alternative engagement. I have had to refuse Coventry for one. A messenger can be despatched post-haste to inform of the vacancy. All I would ask is that you reimburse our fares from Edinburgh to here and I will consider our contract null and void."

M'Cready was a very experienced manager and thought there must be something in the boy if his father was so ready to throw up ten pounds a night so easily. "Pray do not be too hasty, Mr Betty. I am sure we can come to some better arrangement. I propose a variation in the contract. The expenses of the house are sixty pounds each night. I suggest that once this sum has been deducted from the takings, the remainder should be shared equally between us."

"What takings do you average here, Mr M'Cready?"

"Between eighty and a hundred pounds is not unusual, sir."

"Very well. I agree to those terms provided Master Betty also has a clear benefit."

"I will agree to that, providing one of the ordinary nights is given gratis. Shall we say the seventh night? The ninth night for the benefit?"

"Agreed." The men shook hands and the engagement went ahead.

Young Roscius made his first appearance in England on 13th August 1804 and opened with his star role – Norval in *Douglas*. The takings were a disappointing £76.6.0 so, after deducting the £60 expenses, the Bettys' share was only £8.3.0. However, the news of Master Betty was soon disseminated by means of the newspapers and on his second night he gave his Rolla to £117.3.0. He played Hamlet three times bringing in £95.8.6, £170.14.0, and £222.13.0. At M'Cready's entreaty, on the gratis night he repeated his Norval and this time the box-office took £193.9.6.

Soon the hotels and inns of the town were filled to capacity with visitors from outlying parts flocking to see the much-trumpeted prodigy. The Bettys had been booked for thirteen performances which would have originally made them £130 but, as a result of Mr M'Cready's own suggestion, they made well over £500 and Master Betty's benefit alone raised £261.5.6.

William did not understand all that. He just wanted enough money to send back to his mama in Edinburgh. His father assured him he was sending lots of money home. This pleased William because his mother always complained they never had enough. Mr Betty's linen mill never made much money and now, being neglected by his absence, was running at a loss. Mrs Betty knew they were not as well-off as they appeared and it was hard to keep up appearances. She did not like her son being away from home and she hated and strongly disapproved of his appearing on the stage. She accused her husband of turning their son into a vagabond. Mr Betty laughed when she said that, saying he would be the richest vagabond in the world.

But William worried. He was a serious boy and worried that people might stop coming to see him. Then they would be without money again. But, if he mentioned these fears to his father, Papa just laughed and said "There's plenty more where that came from."

On his final night he gave his Richard III and brought £268.4.0 to the box-office. Mr M'Cready was exceptionally pleased with his bargain even though he would have made far more by the original agreement. Over the Bettys' stay he had become very friendly with Mr Betty and had given that man some very useful tips on how to deal with other managers.

"But think on, Betty, I must have Young Roscius back here

again as soon as possible."

"You have my word. He is fully booked for the next few weeks as you know. Hough is convinced we can land a London contract."

"I am sure you can. I have been doing my best for you. The scouts are out, Betty, have no fear of that. You will get London offers. My advice to you is to stick out for fifty pounds a night. Don't take less. One of the patent houses will succumb if you stand firm."

"You think so? Fifty pounds? A night? Hough was talking of fifty a week as big money."

"Mark my words, Betty, your small boy is going to be big. Really big."

— M'Cready was the father of the present day Macready whom you so admire.

— Was his son born at that time?

— Oh, yes. Our current dramatic Colossus was around then. He is much of an age as myself. William and I were playfellows together. I remember many a scrape we got into as lads. Oh, the japes we played! Of course he did not act when a boy like I did. He was educated at Rugby. William was to be a gentleman! Later on, as young men, we often acted together. Oh, I could tell you a great deal about William Macready.

But going back to the time of which I speak, he was still a schoolboy. Our fathers got to know each other very well. As the business at his theatre was prodigious, Mr M'Cready was always inclined to further our interests. I was greeted with acclaim everywhere. You will see in my cuttings that at the Doncaster races they were running special coaches to see Master Betty at Sheffield. At Manchester the demand to see me was so enormous that applications for boxes had to be made in writing. Seats were drawn by lot in the presence of two leading gentlemen of the town.

In Liverpool I was alternating nights with the popular comic actor Munden. On his nights the box-office did not even take enough to clear the theatre expenses. Each of my nights broke the house record. I mention these as examples of the extraordinary effect Master Betty created everywhere he went. You will find many instances of the intense excitement I caused. You could just give a few examples picked at random, I will leave it to you. Oh, but do not allude to the death at Durham, that would not be wise.

— Death? Whose death?

— Oh, some unfortunate woman got struck down and trampled in the crush to see me at Durham. Most unfortunate.

SEPTEMBER 1804

The theatre in Durham City was situated halfway up Saddler Street, a cobbled road leading to Palace Green and the Cathedral. The theatre itself stood not on the roadside but down an alley facetiously known as Drury Lane after the site of the principal theatre in the land. Many country theatres were inconveniently situated as they had started out as other buildings, often merely barns that were temporarily converted for the players' visits. Plenty of tiny towns and villages still only had these fit-up premises and the actors who appeared in them were contemptuously known as 'barnstormers' by their more fortunate fellows. Durham City was one of the towns where a permanent theatre had been built although it was still not valued enough to warrant a prominent position in the townscape. It was commonplace for William to find his place of work down an alley, snicket or ginnel. Thus not only the players but the audience too had to make their way down this lonnen – as such alleys were known in that area.

The management had been able to impose a system whereby patrons could be dropped from their carriages at the entrance to the lonnen, then the driver would carry on up the hill to Palace Green where he could wait in file. As each coach followed the same procedure it prevented the mêlée of vehicles trying to go in both directions at once. The coaches remained on Palace Green until the final curtain then they returned downhill again to pick up their passengers at the entrance. It was a reasonably orderly but incredibly lengthy arrangement. People with less grand pretensions would have their coachman drop them in the market place and they would walk the short distance to the theatre. Of course, the majority of the audience were pedestrians anyway.

Nobody was ever quite clear exactly how the accident happened. Some said the unfortunate lady had been trampled under the hooves of a horse after falling whilst squeezing between carriages. Others swore that it had happened in the narrow lonnen; people rushing to get in the theatre had been too pressing in their excitement, the money-taker had been slow and a pressure of people in the confined space had caused the lady to stumble and be killed by human feet. Whatever the truth of the matter, the unfortunate female ended dead but when it was found that she was only a serving-maid at the Three Tuns the matter was soon forgotten.

William's father thought it wise to keep the news from his son but somehow bad news always seems to spread and William could not but hear of it. Being a boy of great sensibility, he was very distressed. He did not want people trampled to death just to see him. He did not like the reports he read of people actually fighting to obtain a ticket for his performances. The death of one of his audience made him feel like a murderer. All this because more people wanted to see him than the theatre could safely hold. Not for the first time he wondered why they could not stay longer in one place. Give everybody in the town chance to come along. He would prefer that, he could stay in each place longer, have some leisure instead of always moving on. Why did they have to keep travelling from town to town? All he did was act, rehearse, travel and sleep. He barely had time to eat or go to the jakes some days. But his father said this was just the beginning; there would be much more fame ahead and much, much more fortune.

Although Mr Betty astutely booked his son into the largest theatres in the largest towns, he did not despise the more modest fees he could extort from small country theatres. If a long journey had to be broken with an overnight stay, then, wherever possible, he contrived to stop where there was a theatre and a single performance played, squeezing thirty pounds from the desperate manager who had to try and balance his books by increasing admission prices whilst not alienating his public.

— I caused a furore everywhere I went. Now this will interest you, Charlie. The only place where I did not sell out instantly was in Norwich. For some reason my week there started with mediocre houses. Then a letter appeared in the local paper accusing Master Betty of not being a real boy at all but actually a full-grown mature woman though of diminutive stature. A copy of the entry in the church register where I was christened had to be reproduced in the paper. After that they flocked to see Master Betty just as they had everywhere else. I say, I hope you can keep up with my rattling along like this, Charlie.

— I can keep up very well. But before we resume, Mr Betty, may I once more ask you not to address me as Charlie. Not even my own mother calls me Charlie.

— Oh? Well, I was only trying to be friendly. That is my nature. And as I am old enough to be your father –

— I do have a father of my own, sir, and he has always addressed me as Charles.

— Very well. I must have taken the wrong idea. I thought Hogarth called you Charlie.

— You are mistaken, sir. Mr Hogarth is my employer. I'm also paying court to one of his daughters, so he's very likely to become my father-in-law. He knows not to call me anything other than Charles.

— Point taken, sir. What do your friends call you?

— My close friends call me Charles too, but as the relationship between you and me is a business one –

— Exactly, business. Can we get on? We have a great deal to get through. Where were we? Oh, yes. In all the towns we played the local gentry took me up. Mr Parker the High Sheriff of Lancashire was particularly instrumental in furthering my career. He was quite a callow young man, about your age, but had many friends among the upper classes. He followed us everywhere. Actually he became somewhat of a nuisance. He kept following us around the country. He would turn up all over the place, throwing receptions and bestowing lavish presents on me. Eventually my father had to turn him away. Mr Parker seemed to think his attentions entitled him to particular favours.

— Particular favours? In what way?

— Mr Parker is not important to my story. Mr M'Cready is — and that good man gave us further contracts at his other theatres.

— Where are we in time now?

— What? Oh, round about the end of September.

SEPTEMBER 1804

The players were assembled in the green-room of the Theatre Royal, Sheffield. This was another of M'Cready's companies and he hoped that Young Roscius would emulate the success he had had at Birmingham and elsewhere. The manager had summoned his players for ten o'clock in order to rehearse *Hamlet* with the visiting star Master Betty. There was much gossip and curiosity as they eagerly awaited the arrival of the prodigy as his fame had, of course, preceded him and everybody in the profession knew that he was surely destined for either the Theatre Royal, Drury Lane or Theatre Royal, Covent Garden which were the most important theatres in London, a goal beyond the aspirations of most provincial players. The younger actors resented Master Betty as some of them had to give up their parts to him. The actor who normally played Hamlet was having to play the lesser role of Laertes, and the actor who usually played Laertes was demoted to several small walk-on parts. The older actors remained aloof, they knew they had grown old in the provinces and lost any chance of achieving fame in London. However, both the old and young ladies of the company were especially excited.

"What's he like?" asked Mrs Barclay.

"Just such a boy as you would imagine," answered the manager, "fair, bright-eyed, intelligent and handsome."

Miss Kitty Sinclair, who was to play Ophelia, could hardly contain herself when Master Betty entered attended by Mr Hough his dramatic tutor. She thought Master Betty was a complete vision of beauty. He bowed in an elegant manner as the theatre manager introduced him and his tutor to the company. Miss Kitty was thoroughly charmed and disarmed.

The manager made the introductions and Mrs Barclay said "As tonight I shall be your mother Gertrude, allow me to give you a kiss." Miss Kitty, who would have loved to have had the nerve to find a similar excuse, quite trembled with delight when they shook hands.

As the morning's rehearsal progressed Master Betty went up in the estimation of the young actors. They realised that he knew his business as well as they and was prepared to work as hard, rehearse as hard as they ever did. This was a new experience for them as they were accustomed to star actors coming to rehearsal merely to tell the manager what was required of the supporting cast in one or two specific scenes and then disappearing until show time. Master Betty rehearsed as thoroughly as though he had been a member of the resident company, or as if he had never played the part before. But Miss Kitty was most alarmed when, in the middle of the rehearsal, Master Betty had so worked himself up in the closet scene that when he cried "On him! On him! Look how pale he grows!" he fainted in the arms of his friend Mr Hough who caressed and soothed him saying he should rehearse no more. Later Mr Hough asked what had moved and affected the dear boy and Master Betty said "I thought I did see my father's ghost."

That night Young Roscius was greeted with acclaim for his Hamlet, and Miss Kitty was thrilled to be sharing the stage with him. However, she was less delighted to see that during the course of the evening Mr Hough was standing in the wings with a glass of rum and milk from which the boy sipped during the course of the play. She was alarmed to see that when Master Betty came off the stage at the end of the performance he was quite exhausted. She thought he was almost totally devoid of sensation.

The following day the company was rehearsing *Douglas* and Kitty noticed that in a break for refreshment Master Betty was taking pills. Mrs Barclay, who was playing Lady Douglas, told her that the boy was fed daily with tonic pills to maintain his vitality, strength and stamina. That night he played Norval and

Kitty thought the picturesque Highland costume showed off his slim graceful figure to great advantage. She thought his features delicate but somewhat feminine; his eyes a lively blue. She was jealous of his long fair hair which hung in ringlets over his shoulders. In the daytime rehearsals these flowing tresses were confined in a comb.

Kitty found Master Betty friendly but distant. He had no conversation in the short pauses during rehearsal. When not required he sat in a corner with Mr Hough and studied his sides. Kitty saw one of his marked sides, with lines for the proper inflection of the voice, and instructions as to action. That night Betty's first speech was heard with a hushed silence from the audience.

Norval finishes his speech with the desire to be a soldier and gain a name in arms. There was a long pause then, as the actor playing Lord Randolph started his reply, he was interrupted by a tremendous burst of applause. The audience was captured. It had seen many a Hamlet before and reserved judgement on Master Betty's rendition but, like the rest of the nation, it could not resist his Norval.

It was not usual for star actors to play every night. The great Mrs Siddons performed only about fifty nights in a year. A London star visiting the provinces would normally perform three times during one week. At Sheffield Master Betty was contracted for fourteen performances over twenty nights, although he was not aware of that. He lived day by day, relying on Mr Hough to tell him what part he had to rehearse and what play was to be performed.

As the company was rehearsing *Barbarossa*, Mr M'Cready came in with another gentleman unknown to Kitty and spoke to Mr Hough. Kitty soon realised the stranger was Master Betty's father as he told his son that he was to perform the following two nights. Mr Betty and the manager then swept out with Mr Hough following protesting. Young Roscius the Gift of God, slumped on a stool, muttered "They may as well kill me now".

— At this point I must explain something to you, Charles. You need not take this down but it is an important historical point and what I have to say will only make sense if you understand the situation. Things are different nowadays, of course, but at that time there were only two London theatres that were allowed by law to show legitimate plays – Covent Garden and Drury Lane. It had all started many years ago when King Charles II had decreed by royal patent that only two theatres should be licensed for dramatic works, meaning plays. Any other theatre in London was only allowed to present musical offerings – opera, burlettas, pantomimes and so on, not proper plays. It is all different now of course – there are a score of theatres in London putting on legitimate drama, but in those days just the two. So that meant an actor was contracted to one house or the other for the season. They had gentlemanly agreements between them not to encroach on each other's companies. That, of course, meant the players were kept in thrall because if they offended at one house the other would not take them up and they would have to disappear into the provinces to work at all. It is necessary that you understand the position.

OCTOBER 1804

In October the Betty entourage played Leicester, with yet another of M'Cready's companies. Betty Senior and M'Cready Senior, as fellow Irishmen with a similar outlook on life, had become very friendly and together they plotted the next move in the career of Young Roscius.

News of Master Betty's extraordinary progress through the provinces had, of course, been carefully monitored from the metropolis and observers had been sent from both Covent Garden and Drury Lane to see if there was anything in the wonder boy, if he would attract the sophisticated theatregoers and, more importantly, make money for them. The spies returned with the news that their respective theatres would be foolish not to take a punt on the lad.

Discreet overtures were made to Mr Betty, who having become bosom pals with Mr M'Cready, discussed the matter with him. It was M'Cready's solemn opinion that Betty should ask fifty guineas a night and a clear benefit, and he should close with whichever of the two houses would agree to those terms. If he could not get that, then he should send them packing and carry on storming the provinces.

Emissaries sent from London were advised of the terms and despatched back to get approval from their masters. First Drury Lane came back; they would offer twenty pounds a night with a guarantee of ten nights plus a clear benefit. Covent Garden proposed thirty pounds a night for twelve nights plus, of course, the clear benefit. The negotiators came and went. Letters flew back and forth between London, Leicester and Birmingham. Eventually Mr Harris of Covent Garden agreed to the terms that Mr Betty had stuck out for – six hundred pounds to cover twelve performances at a rate of three per week for four weeks plus a clear benefit which was likely to bring in a minimum of a further one hundred pounds. The contracts were signed.

Mr Sheridan of Drury Lane was furious; he had failed to win the prize and immediately despatched a new negotiator to try and woo Mr Betty to break his contract.

"Sir," said Mr Betty to the emissary, "as a man of principle I could not possibly do that. I am sure if Mr Sheridan had a contract with me he would not care to see it broken in such a cavalier manner. However, I do see a way in which I might oblige Mr Sheridan."

At the same terms, he signed for Master Betty to use the three nights which were free from Covent Garden to play at Drury Lane.

Both theatres being in competition to engage his son, Mr Betty had astutely played one off against the other, ending up by getting contracts with both. He realised that, after signing with Covent Garden, the contract did not specify for exclusive services so he was quite legally entitled to engage for the remaining nights.

— It was the first time in the annals of the British stage that any player had been permitted to engage to both houses at the same time. Do you see, Charles, how remarkable that was?

— You've made the situation perfectly clear.

— For that, if nothing else, am I unique.

— You wish me to explain this in your memoir?

— Of course; the situation was quite unprecedented. The gentlemanly agreements had been broken. Now, when we reached Town everybody was eager to gaze upon the marvellous boy. The newspapers had raised the anticipation to fever pitch and trumpeted our arrival. We had gawpers outside the hotel hoping to catch a glimpse of me. One lady of quality actually bribed the manager to allow her to disguise herself as a chambermaid so that she could get a first sight of me ahead of her friends.

NOVEMBER 1804

Five young ladies of quality met together nearly every day. They met for coffee, for tea, for rides in Hyde Park, for shopping, concerts in pleasure grounds, but mainly for gossip. They were great friends but, as is the way of such groups, it was entirely sustained by the necessity to score off one another. At present they were taking tea and discussing at great length and in great detail the arrival of the infant phenomenon Master Betty into the metropolis. All their information, gleaned solely from the public press, was of a conflicting nature. If the newspapers could be relied upon to print the absolute truth all the time there would only be the need for one newspaper and not the many different titles that appeared in London by morning, evening, weekly and monthly intervals.

One lady insisted that she knew for a fact the marvellous boy was a manly youth whose voice had broken. Another said no he was but a child with a piping treble. They discussed his eyes – variously green, blue, brown and violet but unanimously large and limpid – before passing on to his hair. This was, all agreed, long and flowing; some said wavy, some said curly but disagreed on colour. Was it blond or auburn? Certainly lighter than darker and definitely not black. They settled on light auburn. They then discussed the clothes that Young Roscius wore when not strutting the stage, but here their imaginations could run riot as, apart from being in the height of fashion, he would have a myriad of outfits that would encompass every colour and style.

Through all this Lady Danby had been unusually muted. When she thought the time was right she delivered her bombshell. "You can conjecture all you like, ladies, but I can tell you for a fact. I have seen and spoken to Young Roscius." Her friends gaped and then started twittering "Do tell!" "How can you?" "Impossible!" One even said "Lying bitch!" Lady Danby smirked and said that she had heard that the Betty entourage was to put up at Brown's Hotel so she had gone to Mr Brown the proprietor and had persuaded him, by means of her position, her charms and her coin, to allow her to disguise herself and masquerade as one of his staff. Thus, dressed in serving-wench's frock, apron and mob cap, face scrubbed free of all paint and powder, she had been permitted to take in a tray with the boy's breakfast.

Her friends squealed with delight and clamoured for details of the encounter. Lady Danby described how the golden youth was reclining by the window perusing a classic text (dress: green velvet with gold brocade trimmings, white pleated stock with jewelled pin). He had bade her "Good morning", remarked pleasantly on the weather (voice: silver trumpet muted by lambswool), run his fingers through his hair (luxuriant, auburn, cascading to his shoulders), and hoped she would be there to serve him for the rest of his stay. As she bobbed her curtsey, he smiled the most charming smile (even pearl-white teeth, dimpled cheek), and opened the door for her with a courtly inclination.

The young ladies were beside themselves with excitement at this news as they were immature and totally shallow in their dearest interests. Lady Danby sat smugly smiling with no conscience at all considering the whole tale was a collection of untruths. She had indeed played the part of the waitress but she was, in fact, bitterly disappointed to find that the boy had obviously dragged himself from bed still half-asleep and was slumped staring into space in an enveloping dowdy mouse-coloured dressing-gown dragged over his nightgown. His hair was gathered up and pinned with a comb and he was a thin, pale boy of a similar age to her nephew and even less prepossessing. He had not spoken at all, never even looked up, and a man within the room had relieved her of the tray, thanked her, and closed the door after she left.

The whole encounter had taken less than a minute and Lady Danby was left in the corridor staring at an oaken door.

However, she could not tell her friends all this as they did not want truths, they wanted heroes. Thus the group of frivolous friends received the imaginative version with an almost orgasmic ecstasy and, before going their separate ways, made plans to send their servants to each other to arrange their visit to Master Betty's debut appearance.

— We went to see the play at Covent Garden and had no sooner taken our places than I was instantly recognised and mobbed. We had to flee for our very safety. Eventually the Box Keeper came to our rescue and we were escorted to Mr Harris's private box where I was able to remain unseen. This before I had even made my debut. The next night we went to Drury Lane to see the play there and the same thing happened. Only much worse. We were really in the greatest danger from the pressing of the crowds. I found it most alarming; after all I was only a small boy.

— It seems unwise that having suffered at one house your father took you to the other in similar circumstances?

— You can have no conception of the lengths to which the public went just to see me. The public reaction verged on insanity. The day I made my debut at Covent Garden the crowds started gathering at ten o'clock in the morning.

— Really? What date was this?

— We are now at Saturday 1st December 1804 – the most momentous day in the history of the British stage. I was to make my London debut in *Barbarossa*.

DECEMBER 1804

The popular opera *The English Fleet* had been scheduled for Saturday 1st December 1804 but the management of Covent Garden decided to put that aside to bring forth a much greater and newer novelty. On this change of plan the following squib appeared in some of the newspapers:

> What great Bony has often despaired of effecting,
> Little Betty has done, when folks least were expecting;
> 'Tis the talk of the gazers, who loudly repeat,
> He has forced from its station the great English Fleet.

Master Betty was to make his debut in the part of Achmet Selim in *Barbarossa*.

The queues started forming at midday. By one o'clock they had become massive. The theatre doors were not due to be opened until six. Covent Garden was a large theatre and had recently been completely altered to increase the capacity. It now held some three thousand people distributed in a pit, three circles of boxes, a two-shilling gallery and a one-shilling gallery. The architect had allowed for fourteen inches per person on the backless benches throughout. The gathering crowds gave every indication that the capacity limit would be well exceeded.

When the doors were opened at six the air was filled with shrieks and cries. People were fainting from the crush. The house was filled within minutes. Many gentlemen paid box prices, rushed into the boxes then jumped over the balconies into the pit. The theatre was soon full, yet still people pressed in. A force of soldiers was summoned and commanded to stop the doors to prevent further entry. Police were called but intruders held their seats by main force and people who had secured those places weeks before could not gain entrance. Nothing could be done. The pit was a struggling mass as in a surging sea. People fainted in the heat of the pit and had to be passed up to the boxes then out into the lobbies to gain air. The manager raised the curtain a little off the stage in an attempt to issue cool air into the auditorium. There was no possibility of starting the play until some kind of order was restored. Delays were inevitable, the heat building up and tempers becoming more and more frayed. Backstage William was in his dressing-room cowering in terror. He protested to his father that he was ill and could not go on. He tried to go through his lines and found he had forgotten them. Forgotten the lines he had said dozens of times before. He felt sick and sought the bucket that Mr Hough had considerately placed to hand.

Eventually the proceedings started and Charles Kemble went on to commence the specially-written prologue. He was not listened to. The people wanted Master Betty and nobody else was to be suffered. Abandoning his attempt at eulogising the youth in verse, Kemble got the play started and the actors went through Act One in total bedlam. As acting manager that evening, Mr Charles Kemble went on to remonstrate with the audience but he went unheard and retreated in failure. William's character Selim does not come on until Act Two and William, trembling with fear, wondered how he was going to quell the multitudinous rabble.

"I must go to the jakes again. I'm cold. I can't stop shivering. They are not listening to the play. They didn't listen to Mr Kemble. What will they do when I go on? They won't listen to me. They won't be able to hear me. They're making noise all the time. I feel sick. Where's the bucket gone? I can't go on. I'm frightened. I'm frightened."

Master Betty made his entrance. He was dressed as a slave – white linen pantaloons, a short close russet jacket trimmed with sable, and a turban hat. The applause was such as had never been heard in any theatre in the land. Then, as he moved forward to speak his lines, an instant hush fell about the house.

He could do no wrong. His every speech was greeted with cheers, the Prince of Wales himself leading the applause. His every entrance called forth frenzied acclamation. At the fall of the curtain he was called for again and again. Even when he had finally withdrawn, many noblemen and ladies of quality struggled through the crowds to try and go round to see him backstage. The ladies were fainting with ecstasy and the gentlemen wished to shake his hand. In short, Young Roscius had triumphed.

In his dressing-room three figures clutched each other in an embrace and danced around. Mr Betty bellowed with elation "We've done it! We've done it! Champagne! Send for Champagne! We must toast our triumph!" Charles Kemble pushed his way in followed by a motley assortment of actors, audience and newspaper writers. For a short while it was a clamorous bedlam until Mr Hough managed to abstract William from the mêlée and, hastily wrapping him in a greatcoat, bundled him into a waiting carriage that sped them back to their accommodation. Mr Betty was rather annoyed to find his son had made off. The boy had not changed but had fled in his stage costume. And all these people wanted to meet him. He should be there enjoying his triumph. Hough, of course. Always nattering and protecting. William must be made to realise that his career relied on the goodwill of these people and they must not be alienated. But he did not have time to think as he was talking to ten people at once, accepting invitations, gathering up the cards that were presented and luxuriating in his position as the father of Young Roscius.

— What happened at your debut?

— Young Roscius had the most utter and perfect triumph. The next day I was the rage of London. *The Morning Post* of Monday 3rd December devoted half its issue to me. A scurrilous engraving entitled *Theatrical Leap Frog* started circulating. It showed Master Betty leap-frogging over a caricature of John Philip Kemble dressed as Hamlet. Kemble loathed that. All the people of quality rushed to invite us to their houses. It was one party after another.

Mr Parker — the man who followed us everywhere — commissioned both Opie and Northcote to paint my portrait. Now this will interest you, Charles. Our King, when he was Duke of Clarence, was actually present while Northcote painted me. He kept me amused while I was sitting. You are not likely ever to be painted but take it from me — it is a very boring business. The Duke made rude but very funny remarks about the artist. He said that Mr Northcote should use his beard for a paintbrush! Northcote became so angry that he actually turned the Duke out of his studio! Imagine that now — turning out the future King of England! And imagine a humble body like me having the King as an old play-fellow! Oh, yes, I have known the very highest in the land.

You should make the most of my friendship, Charles, it is likely to be the nearest you will get to the mighty in our Kingdom. I do believe there is not a great house in all of London where I have not declaimed in the salon.

— Well, I suppose your mother was proud of you, showing you off in all the grand houses.

— Actually my mother was ill-at-ease with the kind of casual conversation that was indulged in by the ladies of quality. My mother is from a genteel family of ancient stock but is more used to the ways of the country. She frowns at the manners of the fashionable ladies. At that time my new baby sister occupied her. My father and I attended as a twosome. He was always at ease anywhere. He could talk to a prince as easily as to a footman.

— You gave recitations at these functions?

— Alas yes. I hated reciting in drawing-rooms but the ladies would usually press for it no matter how much I protested and my father was always willing to oblige.

— Your father recited too?

— No, no. You mistake my meaning. I mean my father would oblige the ladies by calling upon me. I felt that I was once again in my mother's drawing-room back home in Ireland. Much grander surroundings, of course, but much the same tittering and clucking matrons cooing over me as though I were some specimen to be examined. I was an actor now; my place of work was on the stage not in people's homes.

— Didn't he realise you disliked it?

— Of course; but it was understood that I must do whatever my father desired of me. I was always a dutiful son and I was fully aware of how my father was doing his best for the family. Mr Parker suggested a trust fund be set up for my future under the Prince of Wales and the Lord Chancellor. It was not his place to interfere, of course. My father and I had a private joke – we called the interfering chap Nosey Parker. Parker's idea caused some of the gentry to express concern about my education. Some people felt that I was a national treasure and should be protected. It was proposed that my father withdraw me from the stage and that I should be educated as befits a gentleman, returning later to the stage when I was older.

— And presumably wiser. What did your father think to that?

— He was obliged to issue a statement in the papers saying that he was fully aware of his responsibilities as a parent. I was taken apart from him and spoken to by Lord Eldon himself who explained that I could be put under the protection of the Court of Chancery. I thought that meant I would have to leave my parents and I did not want to do that. Some well-meaning people feared that I was being forced upon the stage against my will.

— And were you?

— Not at all. I was loving every minute of it. Would any child prefer pouring over Latin primers under the gaze of a schoolmaster with a cane, to the adulation and wealth that I was receiving? Of course not. It was one round of parties, balls and carriage rides. Oh, I had a glorious time. Ladies of quality would fondle me and say flirtatious things to me. Some tried to kiss me but I would not permit that. I was too old for such nonsense. Do you know, gentlemen vied with each other for the privilege of visiting my dressing-room after the performance to see my father rub down my sweating body with warm towels. They tried to outdo each other with verses in my praise. They harped on the graceful play of my limbs, my air of intelligence, my fine blue eyes and flowing golden hair, my delicate features, my sweetness of manner, and so on and so on.

DECEMBER 1804

Sir Edward Wolsingham and his new dearest friend Mr Hipton applauded enthusiastically as Romeo committed suicide and reclined decorously on the stage awaiting Juliet's awakening. They were as much taken with Young Roscius as the rest of the Town. They might have been slightly disillusioned if they had been aware that Young Roscius was lying there thinking of nothing more uplifting than his supper awaiting back at the hotel. When the curtain fell they were amongst the first to leap up and push their way out of the auditorium.

"Come on, Hip, quickly!" cried Sir Edward. Sir Edward, having been to see Master Betty before, knew the form. Mr Hipton had only recently been introduced to Bettymania by his new, but very close, friend and was eager to be guided by him. "This way, I know a short cut." Sir Edward pushed open a small door disclosing a steep flight of stone steps. He rushed down them, Mr Hipton close at heel. The two men emerged at the corner of the boxes' vestibule and dashed out into Vinegar Yard ahead of most of the now departing audience, past the King's Entrance, to the house stairs which led up to the green-room and the dressing-rooms above.

"Good evening, Sir Edward," greeted the stage-door keeper, recognising him, and the men were allowed to proceed after Sir Edward had flipped him a coin. Gaining the dressing-room of Young Roscius, Mr Hipton was amazed to find a clutch of men already there and others pressing in behind them. They had all come to gaze at the wondrous boy after his exertions. William's father was rubbing down his naked sweating body with hot towels.

The men of high fashion gushed and twittered, cooed and

postured. One or two poetasters recited their latest effusions about Young Roscius, receiving applause from those who bothered to listen.

"O beauteous vision sent by God, omnipotent deity,
A golden youth of silver voice, harbinger of piety.
Hebe's child, he rides Phaeton's chariot above;
A second Hyacinthus and Apollo's love!"

fluttered one gentleman with rather too much rouge on his cheeks and a partiality to hearing his own voice.

Other gentlemen pressed invitations on to Mr Betty. Their parties, balls and routs were now incomplete without the presence of Master Betty, the new phenomenon of the age. Gradually the group broke up as the gentlemen of fashion left to go to supper, or to a gaming house, or even to return to their homes.

— Now what else is of interest? Ah, yes. On the very day after my debut Buonaparte was crowned Emperor of the French by the Pope and nobody noticed. The *Morning Post* allotted half of all its pages to my debut. Buonaparte was dismissed with a mere inside paragraph. Which showed how much the British public cared about foreign princes!

— Editors always give prominence to the most important news.

— Now the next thing of interest. Remember, that all this time my triumphs were taking place nightly at both theatres. I never played to less than capacity at either house. In fact I can claim to have played to more than the capacity at Drury Lane! You see, on one occasion they removed the doors at the back of the circle and arranged some extra seats on a platform in the lobby so that people could sit and see the stage through the doorways over the heads of the audience.

— The next thing of interest?

— I fell ill.

— Oh, dear!

— Yes. I became seriously ill and my father had to cancel all my appearances. In fact my life was in mortal danger for several days. All London tiptoed.

— All London tiptoed? Indeed? All London tiptoed.

DECEMBER 1804

William was clearly ill and even his father was concerned when Mr Hough suggested that he may have killed his son through overwork. The doctor said William must stay in bed and Mr Betty must cancel all his contracts until further notice. He said the boy was at a stage in his growth where the body required much energy and he had over-expended this energy by his tremendous workload.

Mr Wroughton, the prompter at the Theatre Royal Drury Lane went before the curtain, "Ladies and Gentlemen, I am obliged to read two notes. The first is from Mr Betty the father of Young Roscius: 'It is with profound regret that I state that Young Roscius is unable to appear before you tonight. He has been taken ill with a malady of such severity that it would be dangerous for him to even rise from his sick-bed. He craves the well-known indulgence granted to all players who are enforced to break their contract with the public through no fault of their own. I am your most obedient servant W.H.Betty.'"

The rumbling of discontent that issued from the disappointed audience during the reading of this missive was stilled when Mr Wroughton continued "The second note is from Dr Pearson, a physician known to many of you: 'I have examined the boy actor Master Betty and he is suffering from an acute illness that is causing respiratory complications and extreme lethargy. It is my opinion that the illness has been brought on by a recent excessive workload at a time when his undeveloped body has exhausted all its energy. To avoid a total breakdown of the nervous system I recommend that Master Betty not undertake any further engagements until further notice and that he should remain in bed in the immediate future. Dr D G Pearson.'"

At this news cries of lamentation arose as Master Betty's admirers realised that their idol would not appear before them for some considerable time. Mr Wroughton sought to assuage their disappointment by adding "And now, ladies and gentlemen, in order to prevent uncertain expectation, or future disappointment, I am instructed to say that, with a view to a perfect re-establishment of his health, the Young Roscius will certainly not appear again at this theatre until after the Christmas holidays; the proprietors being determined to look to his health as their first object. I am confident that a generous public, whatever may be their temporary disappointment, will approve and sanction the motive which suggests this precaution."

This statement was greeted with a round of approving applause and Mr Wroughton concluded "If you wish to leave the theatre at this point your admission charge will be refunded but if you remain, in just a few minutes we shall commence a substitute programme starting with the popular comedy of *The Wonder*. I thank you."

William spent all the time in bed. His mother fussed over him, urging her husband to take them all back home to Ireland. She said that her husband had brought William to London on two contracts worth six hundred pounds each and they should now return home as soon as they had been completed.

Both theatres were obliged to issue statements about the non-appearance of Master Betty, while Mr Betty had the certificates from Doctors Blain and Pearson copied to prove that he had to cancel dates because of illness. For several days the newspapers reported his life was despaired of, and all London awaited the latest news with bated breath. Mr Betty arranged for the road outside the house to be covered with straw to muffle the wheels of passing vehicles so that the patient would not be disturbed. All the ladies and gentlemen of fashion sent daily to enquire how he fared. William was under observation by the two doctors, and the Prince of Wales himself sent his own physician. The doctors called twice daily and more if there was an extra flare-up of concern. To stem the press of enquiries Mr Betty had the doctors' bulletins copied and nailed to the door in exactly the same manner as they did for seriously ill royalty.

Unpleasant rumours arose and a growing number of people were suggesting that the boy's illness was, in fact, extreme fatigue caused by the cupidity of his father. Eventually, on the advice of Mr Hough, Betty Senior wrote to the newspapers:

> Sir,
>
> Most of the daily papers have, within these few days, teemed with paragraphs and letters, addressed to me, as the father of Master Betty. Some of them have assumed the gentler shape of admonition; others the more positive form of accusation and censure. I am advised by some to be particularly mindful of my son's health. I am accused by others of wantonly impairing it.
>
> When I consider the motives that have influenced the writers of these letters and paragraphs, it is impossible for me to feel any sentiment of anger. But I own I am hurt by them, and I think I have some little reason to complain. I hope a father may claim to be readily believed, when he asserts that he is tenderly solicitous for the welfare of his son; that he is deeply anxious for his health; and that he is ardently desirous of promoting, to the utmost of his power, his fortune and his fame.
>
> Of the causes that produced my son's frequent appearance at Covent Garden theatre last week, it is not necessary here to enter into any explanation, as they cannot operate again. But upon the state of my son's health, it may afford pleasure to the public to know, that all accounts of his labouring under a severe cold, of his being languid from too great fatigue and exertion, and

of his being under a course of recruiting medicine, are entirely without foundation. His mother and myself never recollect his health and spirits to have been better than they are at present.

Sir, it cannot but be painful for a parent to feel himself under the necessity of making stipulations with the public, that he will not be a careless and negligent guardian of his son. In any other case such a necessity would imply suspicion of the father – in the present I am aware that it has been produced merely by solicitude for the son. Under this impression, I can have no objection to pledge, in the most solemn manner, that, whilst I will use every means to prevent my son from injuring his health by too great and frequent efforts of his, I will take care that the fortune and fruits of his efforts shall not be destroyed nor impaired by any improper conduct or negligence of mine.

Those who know me, would not dream any such stipulation or pledge necessary – but how small must be the number of those persons, compared with the vast mass of the public!

I am, Sir, your most obedient servant,

W. H. Betty

Fortunately the care of the doctors and the prolonged bed rest soon caused an improvement. William asked his father to come and see him and, when that concerned papa bent over to hear his son's feeble words, William said "When I've earned the twelve hundred guineas can we go home?" Mr Betty laughing heartily said "Nonsense!" and that his mother had been getting at him with her moaning. As Mr Betty pointed out to his wife, their place was in Shropshire not Ireland. They would buy a farm or a grand house in the area from whence Mrs Betty hailed and there they would put down roots. There was no future in Ireland. Mr Betty swore that he would space out Young Roscius' future engagements. He was constantly surprised that neither his wife nor his son could appreciate their amazing good fortune and the extent of the wealth flowing into the family coffers.

The people of quality competed with each other to have Young Roscius at their homes to convalesce. A number of lords and ladies begged the Betty family to go and stay with them for William's recuperation. Eventually Mr Betty chose to stay with the Duke of Clarence at Bushy Park and the man who would eventually be the King of England humbly undertook to follow the regime as set down by physicians to ensure William had the right food and fresh air.

— All the ladies and gentlemen of the nobility sent to enquire about me. Fortunately I soon recovered.

— And no doubt all London could walk properly flat on their feet again.

— The future King of England was to follow my physicians' instructions. It is not every man who can claim His Majesty as his nurse.

— First play-fellow, now nurse. How privileged you must have been. How long were you absent from the stage?

— A month.

— A whole month? Your admirers must have been bereft.

— My return was a gala occasion attended by all the royal dukes and the King and Queen themselves. My original contracts had been extended and I was playing at both theatres until the end of the season in May. At Drury Lane the takings never fell to less than five hundred pounds a night. My two benefits alone at that theatre brought me two thousand five hundred pounds. I was responsible for adding forty thousand pounds to the theatre coffers in three months. There is no question but that I saved Drury Lane from bankruptcy. And Covent Garden was in not much better state. My money had risen to a hundred pounds a night. And do not forget, I was still a thirteen-year-old boy.

— At that age I was earning twelve pence a day in a shoe-blacking factory.

— But alas, you are not a genius, Charles. Mrs Siddons herself could not command anything like the money I was paid. John Philip Kemble the head of the profession – much like Macready is today – only earned thirty-seven pounds ten shillings a week. Kemble and Mrs Siddons were brother and sister. Both of them refused to perform during my season. They were afraid of me, you see. They had ruled the roost so long that they were jealous of Master Betty and his popularity. Imagine how they would have felt going onstage to face a half-empty house knowing that only the previous night Master Betty had packed the place from floor to ceiling. They had no intention of risking that. But one person you must mention is Gentleman Smith.

— Gentleman Smith?

— Yes, he was an old actor from Garrick's day, long retired from the stage. I believe he married an heiress and lived in a grand manor somewhere in the country. He had been given a ring by Garrick who instructed him not to hand it on until he saw a player who acted from nature and from the heart. He presented it to me with a poetic effusion. Thus I felt that the great Garrick himself had endorsed me as his natural successor.

FEBRUARY 1805

Mr Betty regularly corresponded with his friend Mr M'Cready the manager at Birmingham, keeping him informed of all that was happening in London. The two men had already agreed that Master Betty's next out-of-London engagement would be a return to Birmingham. Rather than the mere nine months that had actually elapsed, it seemed a much longer time since Mr M'Cready had been so doubtful of the boy that he wanted to cancel his contract. M'Cready was an astute but wily man and he suggested to Mr Betty that some sort of testimonial dinner should be arranged when they eventually arrived. It would attract all the local gentry and ensure full houses throughout the engagement. Mr Betty thought a dinner an excellent idea but could see no reason to wait for Birmingham; the boy should be given one here in London.

So, with the assistance of some gentlemen playgoers, the idea was disseminated that a dinner should be organised to honour the young star. This took place on 27th February and it was arranged that William Smith, an actor who had been in Garrick's company and had retired in 1788 to become a country gentleman in Bury St Edmunds, should be present. Universally known as Gentleman Smith because of his educated demeanour and elegant dress, but most importantly for possessing an aristocratic wife, he had created the role of Charles Surface in *School for Scandal* although being mainly known for playing tragedy. He had been Mrs Siddons's first Macbeth and had alternated Hamlet and Richard III with Garrick himself. As Smith was keen to boast to Master Betty, he had never played in farces or roles that required him to black-up his face or fall through a trapdoor.

Gentleman Smith, who had been entrusted by Garrick with a precious heirloom in the form of a ring, presented it to Master Betty with a lengthy self-penned verse that concluded

"And now when death dissolves his mortal frame,
His soul shall mount to heav'n, whence it came,
Earth keep his ashes, verse preserve his fame."

which brought shouts of acclaim and loud huzzahs.

Mr Brummell, who chaired the dinner, pointed out to William that he could now claim that the great Garrick himself had endorsed him as his natural successor.

— One thing I would like to mention particularly, Mr Betty, is a summary of the roles you played. You keep mentioning the same plays – *Douglas, Barbarossa, Romeo, Hamlet.* What other parts did you play?

— I did Frederick in *Lovers' Vows* , Osman in *Zara,* of course, Tancred in *Tancred and Sigismunda.*

— Were these popular plays?

— Popular at the time. Of course, not many of them are done today.

— Except Shakespeare. He retains his popularity.

— The Bard is always in demand. Hamlet and Romeo were in my repertoire throughout my entire career from beginning to end.

— Yes, you have often alluded to them, but did you ever essay other Shakespearean roles?

— I even displaced Cooke to play Richard III.

MAY 1805

"Good of you to come in, Mr Cooke," said John Philip Kemble rising to greet and shake the hand of his colleague George Frederick Cooke.

"When my manager summons me I have a duty to obey," replied Cooke with a flourish.

"I feared you may be indisposed."

"Indisposed? Why should you fear that, sir?"

"Because you were unable to fulfil your obligation the night before last."

"Ah, a matter of personal regret I assure you, Mr Kemble. Yes, I did have a recurrence of my old complaint. But pray rest assured I shall apologise to my public tonight."

"Who will forgive you as they have so often before."

Cooke placed his hand on his heart and gave a small bow. "My public is very loyal and indulgent to my infirmities."

Kemble, who knew his man of old, did not wish to pursue this line. It was true that Cooke had a loyal following. He had been leading man at Covent Garden when Kemble was leading man at Drury Lane. They had been rivals but when Kemble had bought into Covent Garden three years previously they had perforce become colleagues. Kemble was no fool and realised that in several roles the public preferred Cooke to himself. After a period when the two men had come in turn before the public as Richard III, which was Cooke's principal part, Kemble had astutely given way as it was obvious he was outclassed. He settled for playing Richmond to Cooke's Richard. In recompense Cooke was obliged to cede Hamlet to Kemble and settle for the Ghost in future. Thus the two men had mollified each other at the beginning of the new Kemble regime.

In spite of all that, Kemble had to fill two conflicting positions. As well as being leading actor he was also the manager. These two duties often tore him apart. As a manager he had to do all he could to keep money flowing into the coffers and thus was compelled to put on popular farces, pantomimes and other novelties which he, as an actor, disdained. It was bitter gall for the country's leading tragedian to see vast amounts of the theatre's budget going to the father of a mere spouting boy who had caught the fancy of the fickle public pulse.

"I trust you have not summoned me merely to heap coals of obloquy on my contrite head?" asked Cooke.

"It is a completely different matter I wish to see you about, George," replied Kemble in what he thought was a companionable manner between equals. "As you know I always announce your Richard for Mondays – "

"Rest assured I will be there on Monday next – "

"Alas, no. That is what I wish to discuss – er, inform you about."

"I am not to give my Richard next Monday?"

"No. Master Betty will essay the role that night," replied Kemble with some discomfort.

"Master Betty?" Cooke leapt to his feet with outrage.

"Sit down, George, sit down."

"The idea is risible."

"I quite agree."

"Well you are the manager – you must not permit it."

"I am the manager but I am not the owner. I have but one sixth of the patent. Mr Harris owns half and so can out-vote me every time, in any matter. Mr Harris desires Master Betty to give his Richard."

"Mr Harris is a barbarian," said Cooke.

"It is well-known that we players always dislike our managers. Mr Harris does many things I like, several things I heartily dislike. But always his first duty is to keep the theatre solvent."

"Pah! Always the same – money must take precedence over art!"

"Yes, well, this is not the time or place to debate the matter. Mr Betty Senior wishes his son to play Richard so you, my dear fellow, must relinquish the role for one night at least."

"So this is to be a permanent reduction to my repertoire?"

"Not at all."

"Richard is the brightest jewel in my crown."

"And so it shall remain. I do not think Master Betty as Richard will take with the public. He has not essayed the role before in London. It is way beyond the lad's capabilities. The public will only stand so much humbug."

"The boy is nothing in any role but has achieved public acclaim in them all!" expostulated the outraged Cooke.

"The parts he plays had been carefully selected by Hough. He trained the boy in them by simplifying the effects. Hough has gone and Betty Senior is in total control. His demands are getting more and more outrageous. Mr Harris is currently negotiating terms for next season and I will not insult you by naming the sums being discussed. It is all a bubble, George. It will burst sooner or later. This appearance as Richard may be the thing that pricks the bubble."

Cooke thought about it. Kemble could be right. The boy was talented to a degree. He could spout verse, he had a pleasing person – but all players, except a few susceptible very young actresses and some matronly ones, knew he could not act. Perhaps in ten years he would be a rival but at present he was but a schoolboy skilled in elocution. Cooke had played Lord Glenalvon to Betty's Douglas; he had felt the warmth and approbation that the audience had bestowed on the boy; he did not dislike him but, as most actors, he was jealous of the boy's success. If you could believe the rumours, they were now paying Betty a hundred pounds a night whereas he, after toiling five years at the Garden, was still on fourteen pounds a week and his last benefit night had only brought in two hundred pounds.

"As I have no choice, I accept your decision, Mr Kemble," said Cooke rising.

"There is one more thing, George," said Kemble hesitantly.

"Yes?"

"Mr Betty has asked that you undertake Buckingham."

Cooke's eyes bulged and he slumped back in the chair gasping for breath. "You deliberately insult me, sir. The suggestion is monstrous!"

"You will not do it?"

"Most decidedly not! I am appalled you should even ask it of me!" gasped Cooke who was, in truth, not a well man. That summer he had had a ruptured blood vessel in his chest and had been unable to work for a month. His liver too was in poor shape caused by the inordinate amount of alcohol he regularly consumed.

"I told Mr Harris I did not think you would agree to it. Do not worry yourself about it, George. I only broached the subject on Harris's particular insistence. He seems so in thrall to Betty that he wishes to indulge the man's every whim. Of course it is an insult to you. Hough would have known it was an insult but I fear Betty is very unworldly and is blind to the effect of the excessive efforts he is making to promote his son."

"I am in pain, Black Jack. You have cut me to the quick."

"Forget it, George. The fact you are not giving your Richard on Monday next will be put down to your infirmity. It will be announced well in advance so your public will not be disappointed. You keep well away from the theatre."

Cooke rose to his feet. "Cooke does not make pretend excuses. Tell Mr Harris – Cooke will not take second place to any man much less a mere boy!" Striding to the door, he opened it with a flourish and stormed out.

Kemble sighed. The deed was done. He knew it was fruitless even to suggest that Cooke should take a lesser role. Of course it was an insult. Perhaps the man would resign if insulted enough? Kemble had been trying to get rid of him for years. Ever since he became manager in fact. The trouble was that when sober Cooke was excellent and had a large following. Kemble also realised that in certain parts Cooke was his superior. He had even magnanimously announced in public that, after seeing Mr Cooke play Richard, he would never play the part again. He had tried to get along with the fellow by suggesting they divided the leads between them and Cooke had perforce to agree as Kemble had the whip hand. But over all was Harris. Harris, who had an unaccountable leniency towards Cooke. Harris, who time after time made excuses for the wayward actor and resolutely refused to get rid of him. Kemble was forced to smile when he recollected the many fulminations that Cooke had sent winging round the green-room about their proprietor. The poor fellow did not realise that the man he so vilified was the very man keeping him in gainful employment.

Kemble buried his head in his hands and thought "I have borrowed a good deal of money to buy a sixth of this business. How am I to repay it if Harris's ill-placed lenity to an individual, who through intoxication repeatedly disappoints the public, risks the dilapidation of the theatre? Causes my ruin? It is not to be borne."

There was a tap at the door.

Kemble looked up. "Come!"

The door slowly opened and the head of George Frederick Cooke humbled in. "Except you, Mr Kemble; of course you know I will always support you."

— But Richard was not really right for me. I scored best as either Selim in *Barbarossa* or Young Norval in *Douglas*. They were alike in that I played a young hero who had the sympathy of the audience and I did not have to come on until the second act! Undoubtedly my star part was Young Norval; I rarely omitted that. Have you seen my portrait by Opie? Everybody says it perfectly captures me in the role.

— No, I've not had the pleasure of seeing your portrait.

— An excellent likeness – you can readily see why I was idolised. My father paid a man called Heath to do an engraving from the Northcote painting. It cost him eight hundred pounds but he was able to get that back many times over. He sold prints at half-a-guinea a copy. Hundreds were sold. At that time there was hardly a dwelling in the land that did not have two pictures on the wall – one of Nelson and one of Master Betty.

— Why did you favour that particular role?

— Well the main thing is you do not have to enter until Act Two. The other players have to grind through speeches laying the plot and setting up the situation. Then, in Act Two, Young Norval comes on and gets all the applause.

> My name is Norval: on the Grampian hills
> My father feeds his flocks; a frugal swain,
> Whose constant cares were to increase his store,
> And keep his only son, myself at home.

Ah, yes, an excellent long speech there, then very little else in Act Two. Norval does not appear at all in Act Three. Then there is an excellent speech of some thirty-two lines at the beginning of Act Four. The rest of that act is all the business with my long-lost mother. I really used to get the applause with this:

> Bless'd be the hour I left my father's house!
> I might have been a shepherd all my days,

And stole obscurely to a peasant's grave.
Now, if I live, with mighty chiefs I stand;
And, if I fall, with noble dust I lie.

A real clap-trap speech that, never failed!

— I don't know the play.

— I did not suppose you would. I do not know why it has not kept its place on the stage in London but it is still popular in the provinces. I have taught the role to my son. It was my greatest triumph. Norval, who is the long-lost son of Lady Randolf, dies in the last act. It is a very well constructed piece and whilst allowing the actor playing Norval a great deal of time in the green-room, it gives him all the opportunities on the stage. I met the author Mr Home, you know. He was a very old man by then but he said that my enacting of the role was the finest he had ever seen and was exactly as he had envisaged the part when writing it.

— That was in Edinburgh, I believe.

— Oh, I have already told you that.

— Shall we carry on? Where are we now in your history?

— Well my first triumphant season closed on 23rd May 1805 when I gave my Hamlet at Covent Garden for my final benefit.

MAY 1805

Mr Betty Senior had been very pleased when first introduced to the benefit system. It seemed an excellent way to enhance his son's prodigious income even more. Nobody knew when it was introduced, or by whom, as it had always been there. It was generally supposed that some impecunious manager had devised it as way of persuading actors to take particularly low wages. It worked in this way – an actor contracted with the manager, usually on the basis of a weekly salary and, should he try to demand more money, the manager would say "Of course you will be entitled to a benefit." This being offered by way of compensation. The benefit night could be each season or at each theatre where the company appeared, depending on the agreement between the parties. The principle of the benefit was that, after the expenses of the house had been deducted, the actor received all the takings for that one performance. This, in theory, should have been a large amount and in the case of star performers like Master Betty, John Philip Kemble and Mrs Siddons it was. Popular players made their wealth from touring and their occasional benefit nights when they often pulled in well over a hundred pounds for the night. The star pantomime performer Joseph Grimaldi earned four pounds a week at Drury Lane during the winter season and six pounds a week at Sadler's Wells Theatre in the summer season. Sometimes there was an overlap in the seasons and he was obliged to play at both theatres in one night, often running back and forth the two miles between theatres to fulfil his contracts. But even the busy Grimaldi found time to make a flying visit to places like Rochester and come back with a hundred and fifty pounds in his pocket.

However, in the case of lesser lights, the benefit could actually cost them money as they had to guarantee the expenses of the house. Having been granted a benefit, the player would try and get the support of colleagues by asking if they would take part. It was a lucky player who had a chum who was a popular favourite as his friend's appearance would greatly enhance ticket sales. It was up to the player himself to sell tickets for his benefit and it was often a dispiriting business trailing round town trying to get the support of the gentry for this financially-crucial event. Some players, lowly in the company's ranks, were granted a half-benefit and this meant that two of them would share a benefit night. This, of course, meant they would only get half the takings but the risk too was halved.

Actresses who sold tickets for their benefits often resorted to trailing their children round with them from door-to-door in the hope that the sight of their little offspring would touch the heart of the householders and result in ticket sales. It was often a case that people would take tickets out of charity but did not bother to actually turn up at the performance, perhaps sending their servants instead.

But, of course, all this was totally unknown to Master Betty the Young Roscius. His benefit nights were merely excuses to inflate the normal prices and to take the lion's share of the box-office. Thus it was that his father, when negotiating contracts, always demanded a benefit night. Some of these brought in such spectacular amounts that Betty was able to remember them for the rest of his life.

— My final benefit brought in little short of twelve hundred pounds including presents. My father engaged with both theatres for the next season starting in November at greatly enhanced terms, and I set out for a triumphant tour of the provinces.

— Which towns did you play?

— All the places I had visited on my pre-London tour. There was not one manager who did not beg me to return. But first of all, of course, I gladly performed again at Birmingham. After all Mr M'Cready had been very instrumental in furthering my career.

JUNE 1805

"You know, Betty, you have treasure trove in that boy of yours," said Mr M'Cready.

"Sure and don't I know it," replied Mr Betty. "He's helped to boost your coffers too, M'Cready, don't forget that."

Replete after an excessively good dinner, the two men were enjoying cigars and brandy. Their wives and children were entertaining themselves elsewhere "leaving the men to talk". It had been a most pleasant day, both families had ventured forth to view the progress of the latest canal diggings then proceeded to elevated countryside where they picnicked, flew kites and generally tumbled around. They had a magnificent view over a great part of the city and Mr M'Cready had pointed out the principal manufactories and works. Birmingham had already become the workshop of the world. The drive home was made exciting by witnessing a collision between a brewers' dray and some market stalls, the day concluding with a quite magnificent repast at the M'Cready home.

"I am not talking merely of his phenomenal earning power. I mean he is a really good, talented boy who will do well in whatever line he follows. You see, he takes everything in. He's like a sponge. He doesn't say a lot – he's not a chatterer – but I think we would all be surprised at how much is inside that head. I think he may well turn out to be a very great man."

"But surely he is already destined to be the greatest actor of the age?" protested Betty.

"Come, Betty, he will want to be something better than that. It is well enough now and I admit he is probably the most famous name, and certainly the highest paid player, in the country. But that's only now. This year. Who knows what the future will bring. He will go to university, study wonderful things. Learn about science and inventions. Knowledge, Betty, that's what it's all about."

"I see no necessity for my son to be anything other than an actor. It is an honest living. You, yourself, M'Cready are one. Do you not see honour in your own calling?"

"Oh, come, Betty. I am a mediocre player; that is why I have turned to management. I have no exaggerated ideas about my own talents. I am a business man. I know about the theatre so I have made it my business. If I knew about coal then I would run a coalmine and not a theatre. People must be entertained so I make it my business to entertain them. It is my business. At the moment Young Roscius is what people demand. So I provide it. At a price. We have become close friends, I hope, Betty, but I am under no delusion that you would let me have the services of your son for any lower rate than the highest you could extort. Because you too are a man of business. I will engage your son so long as he draws but, when he ceases to do that, then I must search for another attraction." M'Cready puffed smoke into the air.

"I think you are rather flippant, M'Cready, if I may say so. My son has been hailed by many as a second Garrick. Indeed many have said he exceeds Garrick! He has broken house records everywhere. His two benefits alone at Drury Lane made us almost two-and-a-half thousand pounds."

"Yes, I know all that. You will probably make as much again from your stay here. That is not the point. Let me caution you not to believe all your own ballyhoo."

"My friendship with you leads me to be bold enough to suggest that you may be somewhat jealous of my son's achievements in relation to your own boy's prospects."

M'Cready laughed. "You think I want my son to be a common actor? Nonsense man. William is at Rugby School and will go to Oxford and be something far superior to anything his father has managed. That is what civilisation is all about, Betty. Progress. We oldsters must step back and let the young ones take over, yes, but we must be behind them pushing them along to greater things. Better, more magnificent things. Things that we can only dream of and things that we cannot yet know."

"Well nobody can accuse me of not pushing my son on to greater things."

"No," agreed M'Cready with a twinkle in his eye, "nobody can accuse you of that."

— At Birmingham I received a thousand pounds for thirteen nights playing. I still hold the house record at Durham. The manager said I was the greatest tragic performer who had ever stalked his boards. I broke box-office records everywhere. You would not believe the money we made. We cleared ten thousand pounds from June to November. Everybody clamoured for me. It was one great constant tour that went on and on for six solid months. My father joked that we were like highwaymen. Always on the road and taking money from people.

— Very droll.

— My father worked me very hard on that tour but we did have a lot of fun. There were just the two of us. My father had dispensed with – all employees, and Mother had stayed behind in London with her new baby. My father was always up for some jape or other. I will never forget a night at Minchinhampton. Sometimes, because of the distances between towns, we were obliged to stop for a night at some small country place. My father, loathe to waste these overnight halts, arranged them at towns that had a theatre. Well you can imagine what sort of places they were! But if they paid us thirty or forty pounds for the night we were content. These wretched theatres had to increase their prices, of course, but that did not stop the entire countryside flocking to see me.

We played this benighted place called Minchinhampton because we needed a convenient stop on the journey from Daventry to Bristol. The theatre there had only one dressing-room. There was a closet that the manager used as his personal dressing-room and office, this being allotted to me as the visiting star. The sole dressing-room was used by the ladies of the company, and the men had to change and prepare themselves on the stage itself. Well my father saw this and tipped a stagehand half a guinea to pull up the curtain before time. You have never seen such a display of spindle-shanks and bare rumps exposed to the public gaze! Dad was a great one for japes!

— Do you wish me to include that in your memoirs?

— Good heavens, no! Not at all. We could not have William Macready reading that! That would make him look down his nose and pontificate upon the dignity of his calling! But it was a grand jape all the same. Will you take a bottle of Burton-ale? My throat is quite parched with all this talking. No? Very well. I am sure you will not begrudge me. I see you are perusing my album. You have found something of particular interest?

— A name only. One of your fellow actors. Vincent Crummles. What a magnificent name. I collect unusual names. A writer has to find suitable appellation for his characters.

— I remember Crummles. Excellent actor. Never came to anything. That is the thing you see. Just as I am sure you are a perfectly competent writer and may well in time develop into a good one, actors can be competent, good or even excellent, and still fail. But I was more than excellent – I was a genius. My vocal chords were touched by God.

— And now they are touched by thirst.

— What? Oh, yes – that's a good one. Touched by thirst. Here, take a bottle for yourself. Now where were we?

— On your post-London triumphal tour making a great deal of money.

— Ah, yes. Well, as I say, we made a great deal of money and then it was time to return to London for my second season.

— Didn't you have any respite? No holiday break?

— There was no time for that. So many theatres wanted us we could not fit them all in as it was.

— Right. Second London season now?

— Yes. It was much as the first. More triumphs. As you purport to be a writer you can use your imagination to fill it out, can you not? I played much the same parts. I tried Richard III again. Cooke had to stand down. The old rascal hated that but he was not in a position to do anything about it. Good old Cooke. I really liked the man. Had some character – not like that stuffed shirt Macready. Wishy-washy actor. It is not surprising he appeals to you young fellows nowadays.

— I presume that is not to be written in your memoir?

— Better not. Where was I? Oh, yes, my second season in 1805. Unfortunately, it was at this time that fate conspired against me. If you know your history as, surprisingly, you seem to, you will realise that I was playing when the nation was in mourning for the death of Lord Nelson, slain at Trafalgar. Then both Pitt and Fox died. By February the gaiety of England was plunged into the gloom of war. Our leaders were dying and Napoleon Buonaparte was at our gates. It was a sad time. A sad time.

— What did you do?

— As players have always done. We carried on in adversity. At the end of the season we returned to the provinces. Audiences were still strong there. We toured for several years. People who had heard of Master Betty wanted to see the phenomenon in person. I was now growing rapidly and, to be honest, it was difficult to reconcile myself to being Master Betty for much longer. I was now considerably taller and heavier than I had been on my debut in London, and my voice had broken. During all my touring, barely without realising it, I had turned from a boy into a man. My mother conceived the plan that I should go to university and get an education. We deemed it wise at this point to retire from the stage.

— So your story ends there?

— Not quite, Charles. But there is not much more to cover now. What do you think of my tale, eh?

— It's most uncommon. If it were a work of fiction the author would be accused of hyperbole.

— My story is unique. Of course there have been infant phenomena in other fields. One thinks of Mozart the musical prodigy, Chatterton that marvellous boy poet and, of course, Sir Thomas Lawrence who was supporting his family with his brush when only twelve-years-old. But I think no one in the theatrical world has ever been blessed by God with talents such as mine. Is there anything that you would like to ask me before we proceed? Any amplification of any point? It must be difficult for a man of modest means and attainments to understand the extra-ordinary situation of a prodigy such as myself.

— You've conveyed the adulation you received wonderfully well.

— You will find able assistance from my press-cuttings book. It is very comprehensive. My dear mother, as most mothers, was very proud of her son and garnered every piece of tittle-tattle about me. I do believe you will even find a clipping from *The Sun* printing my height and weight, on the assumption that everything about the Heaven-sent youth was of inordinate interest.

— I find it rather surprising that you, sir, as a boy, played in normal plays with adult actors rather than a piece especially concocted for yourself. Perhaps one better designed to show off your finest skills?

— That is what was so amazing about me, you see. I, a mere boy, was playing the same parts as John Philip Kemble, George Frederick Cooke and all the other star actors. I not only played roles that the great Garrick himself had played but outshone him in them. You will find that in print. Many competent judges, having seen both of us, made that declaration. You will not understand the importance, but you must make that clear, Charles. Not only was I a second Garrick but I surpassed the master!

— You had retired from the stage.

— Ah, yes. I went to university. Did you go to university, Charles?

— No.

— Educated at the University of Life, eh, Charles? My last performance was at Stratford-upon-Avon. Most appropriate that, was it not? The birthplace of the immortal Bard. I gave my farewell as Norval on the 11th July 1808 and the very next day enrolled as an undergraduate at Christ College Cambridge. I was seventeen. I remained there until 1811 when, unfortunately, my father died. I was called upon to return home to care for my mother and sister. My father had taken a lease on a farm in Shropshire. I gradually turned into a country gentleman. I had a commission with the county Yeomanry and I discovered that I had extraordinary skill in the sport of archery. Have you ever tried archery, Charles?

— No.

— No, it is really a sport for gentlemen. Very difficult. Not many men attain my proficiency. I was also a first-class shot with the rifle. It was expected that I would take over from my father at the farm. But I was not happy as a country squire. I believed it was a waste of all my wonderful God-given talents. I retained an ardent love of the profession and felt I still had so much to give to the world. Therefore, in the year 1812 a momentous thing happened.

— It certainly did – I was born.

FEBRUARY 1812

Even when a man already has daughters he is especially pleased at the significance of the birth of his first son and Mr John Dickens was overjoyed when a brother for his beloved daughter Frances arrived lustily into the world. Mr Dickens's parents had been upper servants in a grand house and he had been brought up peering from the edges at wealth and luxury. This had fostered an ambition in him to grow up to be a gentleman and he thought the key to progress for a poor man was to acquire an education. This he had done with some application but being a cheerful, easy-going sort of fellow he did not pursue his educational quest with sufficient ruthlessness. His ambition was, unfortunately, tainted with a dash of fecklessness and his lofty aspirations had become somewhat grounded as a clerk in the Navy Pay Office in Portsmouth. This position he had obtained through the good offices of his father-in-law who, himself, had been employed with the Navy Pay Office until a matter of embezzlement obliged him to precipitously flee the country. Mrs Dickens's parents, however, came from the middle classes and it was generally acknowledged by her family and friends that, regardless of her father's unfortunate brush with the law, she had married beneath her.

But all was happiness and joy within the little family in the tiny terraced house in Portsmouth on 7th February 1812 when Charles John Huffham Dickens entered this teeming world and the *pater familias*, looking at his new born son, made many plans in his head and vowed that, not only would he be a gentleman, but that he would become a Great Man.

Within a few months, however, the family was in upheaval as

they were obliged to move; this would be by no means a rare thing in the young Dickens's life as John Dickens, with his easy-going temperament, was perpetually teetering on the brink of financial embarrassment. The arrival at intervals over the next few years of a further four children, whilst adding to their parents' joy, did nothing to stop the flow of pennies from the family coffers. John Dickens spent his life assuring his wife that something would turn up. In 1817 that 'something' was an increase in salary to three hundred pounds per annum and a move to Chatham when Dickens was transferred to the Naval Dockyard there, the largest in the world.

There Charles had a settled respectable life, his parents being able to afford to take a comfortable house with a garden and employ a couple of staff. Unfortunately, Charles's pretty, vain and vivacious mother was no better at housekeeping than her husband and, even with the enhanced salary, they were obliged to cadge loans from family and friends as they spent what little money they had on entertaining rather than pay the outstanding tradesmen's bills. But a young boy is never aware of his parents' financial affairs and Charles led a carefree and imaginative life.

Never physically robust, Charles's childhood was punctuated with recurring bouts of illness and he read voraciously when confined by ill-health and continued to do so when restored to vigour. His father had a collection of cheap editions of famous novels and Charles devoured the works of Smollett, Fielding and Defoe. To most boys these stories appeared hopelessly old-fashioned but Charles entered into their worlds with a vivid imagination that brought the old tales to life. He came to think of fantasy and fact as one and the same world.

His rudimentary education was provided, as is often the case, by his mother. Later he was a pupil at a local dame school and, when he was ten, attended a school run by a clergyman. His older sister Fanny was a fellow pupil and both brother and sister delighted in reading, writing and music; Fanny, in particular, was considered to be a very promising musician. Charles loved the theatre; Dr Lamert, his uncle by marriage, often took him to the

Theatre Royal in Chatham and he never forgot his terror seeing the evil Richard III fighting for his life against the heroic Richmond. In later years, Charles often wondered if that had been his first sight of William Charles Macready.

John and Elizabeth Dickens encouraged their children in their artistic attempts so the writing and acting of plays became a great part of their happy childhood life. Music, recitations and comic songs were always being performed for family and friends and it would be pleasant to be able to say that this family life continued on its happy way. Unfortunately, in genteel poverty, the privation often outweighs the gentility and once again the Dickens family were obliged to move to a smaller house.

A year later an even bigger blow struck – John Dickens was transferred to Somerset House, the headquarters of the Navy Pay Office in London. The move brought with it a reduction in salary and must perforce be seen as demotion, but beggars cannot be choosers and the easy-going John Dickens went along with it.

To Elizabeth and Charles's disgust, John Dickens could afford to rent only a mean property in Camden Town. The fact that their next-door neighbour was a mere washer-woman indicated the general tone of the area. Charles thought that his chances of becoming middle class – much less a Great Man – were rapidly receding.

— Ah-ha! Of course; you said you were born in 1812. But more importantly, I was re-born. Now being aged twenty, I felt I must return to the theatre.

— Under what necessity?

— No financial necessity. I was a very rich young man. But I had this God-given talent. It was given to me to share with my fellow man. It was almost as though I was defying the Lord not to use it.

— No doubt in your absence from the stage you had received regular pleas from the theatres to make a come-back?

— Exactly. I returned as a duty and was welcomed back at Bath. I received eight hundred pounds for nine nights. Then I accepted an offer to appear at Covent Garden at my old terms of fifty guineas a night.

NOVEMBER 1812

Since the retirement of Young Roscius both Drury Lane and
Covent Garden theatres had burned down and new, more
magnificent buildings, erected in their stead. During the late
destruction of Drury Lane Mr Sheridan was seen in the street
quaffing a glass of wine and, when asked how he could remain
so calm in view of his great calamity, remarked "Surely a man
can have a quiet drink by his own fireside?"

The new theatres were designed to give greater comfort to
the spectators, not only in the passages, vestibules and saloons,
but also much more space was allowed for them in the auditoria
and, whilst the capacities of both houses were still classed as
three thousand persons, those people occupied a much greater
area and the distance from the front of the stage to the back
seats was much further than before. The stages were larger too
with a greater emphasis being put on the spectacle rather than
the speech. At Covent Garden, John Philip Kemble himself was
accused of inaudibility from the one-shilling gallery. On being
told this, he marched to the front of the stage and declared in
ringing tones "They *shall* hear me!"

When, with the opening of the new theatre, the patentees
attempted to recoup building costs by raising the admission
charges in the pit from three shillings and sixpence to four
shillings, and box seats up from six shillings to seven shillings,
the result was sixty-seven continuous nights of rioting when the
audience would not suffer the actors to be heard. Capitulation
came and order returned only when the management restored
the old price in the pit and the theatregoers accepted the new
price in the boxes. In the pit a banner reading "We are Satisfied"

was unfurled and the tumult ceased.

In 1812 the new Covent Garden theatre was three years old when William went into Mr Kemble to sign the contract and discuss the roles he would play. He was not to know that there had not been wholehearted approval from the theatre committee about his engagement but once again bankruptcy hovered and some of the patentees thought that as Master Betty had done the trick before he could probably do it again. Of course, William had said he would play all his old roles. His public expected that. The patentees said that whilst they would certainly also expect that, they pressed the suggestion he also undertook a new role, perhaps Alexander the Great? They knew Mr Kemble had an excellent play on that subject submitted by a prominent member of the committee and thought the part would suit William well. Mr Kemble said he was not sure that William was the ideal player for the part. William replied that, free from vanity, he could honestly apprise his figure as being built of heroic proportions and his looks had matured into handsome features. He considered his voice far more powerful, and assured Mr Kemble that not only would he be able to be heard in the new theatre, he was so well-practiced in his roles that he was able to bring extra emotions and resonances out of the words.

Mr Kemble had grumbled at the terms William proposed but several patentees pointed out that was what he received seven years ago and, after all, when he was Young Roscius he had rescued the theatre from bankruptcy; surely the committee should remember that? So the patentees agreed to be swayed and Mr Kemble was instructed to contract William for twenty-four nights. Privately William thought they should really pay him more now he was a much more proficient, far better actor but, not being a greedy man, he thought it wise not to push his luck. As he pointed out, all he asked was his just deserts.

When William enquired about the dates of his engagement, Mr Kemble replied that the reason for the delay was they were trying to make sure that the Prince Regent and the Duke of Clarence would be free to attend his return to the London stage.

He feared the dear old King would not be well enough. When William protested further, Mr Kemble sought to appease him by putting his first date in the immediate calendar – as Selim in *Barbarossa* – saying he was sure all his loyal followers were looking forward to renewing acquaintanceship with Master Betty. Of course, now being a twenty-one-year-old man, he could no longer be billed as Young Roscius and would go before his public as William West Betty.

— I was received with enthusiastic acclaim and hailed as the British Roscius. I was at the pinnacle of the profession. Now, Charles, be sure to make it clear that I was the leading actor of the day. Macready was nowhere, Kean still unheard of. Betty was the greatest star. You can have no conception of the idolatry that was thrust upon me. You see, Charles, many older people regarded me as a re-incarnation of the great Garrick. Mrs Siddons quailed at my very name. What's this? Why have you thrust this paper on me so unmannerly? Dickens? Dickens? What is this word?

— That is my name! Charles John Huffham DICKENS!

— So? I do not understand?

— Ever since I arrived you have treated me with little more than contempt. In spite of my many protests you insist on addressing me as Charles –

— But you asked me to call you Charles!

— I did not, sir. I strongly objected to being addressed by the ridiculous form Charlie and you promptly presumed to call me Charles.

— Well, I am very sorry if I have been presumptuous. You said your friends called you Charles and I considered, as we were friends, that is how I should address you. No offence was intended.

— I consider our relationship a business partnership, Mr Betty.

— A business partnership. I am a considerably older man than you, sir, and my position in society is, I believe, somewhat above yours, *Mister* Dickens. But I am not a proud or haughty man. I was merely trying to be friendly as I am to all my fellow men. However, as you so wish it, I shall call you by your surname. I think if Mrs Betty were here she would tap you with her fan and say "Young man, you are being hoity-toity."

— I intend no disrespect to you, sir, but I feel respect should be mutual.

— Of course, of course, that goes without saying. May we proceed with our business, *Mister* Dickens?

— You had reached the pinnacle of your profession. Pardon me, sir, but surely the late Edmund Kean had arisen by this time?

— Kean? No, no. He did not make his London debut until the year before Waterloo. But Kean was never hailed as the British Roscius.

— I once saw him as Richard III.

— He got most of that from Cooke. It was Cooke's greatest role. Kean venerated him. When Kean was on form he was a genius. But most of the time he should never have been allowed on the stage. He was far too erratic. He wasted his talents. Kean was born a bastard in a theatrical skip. He was a pantomime child. Learned acrobatics and all that line of business. He was an excellent Harlequin, you know. He spent twenty years struggling in the provinces before he made his debut in London. Then he became a star overnight. But he soon showed his true colours. Became unreliable. Started missing performances and, when he did turn up, he was drunk out of his mind. Then he got involved with that unpleasant adultery case.

— What was that?

— Oh, some alderman took him to court for carrying-on with his wife. Well, the public will only stand so much from its favourites and he started getting booed off the stage. I think some of these players receive so much praise that it turns their heads. They seem to have this overweening pride. They think they are above lesser mortals and that, because of their position, any kind of outrageous and immoral behaviour may be tolerated. Actors should always remember that they are the servants of the public. Kean was a low sort of fellow, forever wenching. He used to actually bring these trollops into his dressing-room and was whoring while the play was on! At bottom Kean was only a jumped-up mountebank. He had his admirers, of course, mainly the left-wing press.

— Did you ever act with him?

— He refused to act with me. I was engaged to play four nights at Stroud. The theatre was a wretched hovel of a place. Kean was their leading man. He was only about twenty years of age and worked for a miserable pound a week. When he was told he would have to step down to support me, he refused! Well, he did not even refuse. He just disappeared. He fled into the open country and lived on turnips and cabbages, filched from farmers' fields, until I had gone. He was a rum cove was Kean.

AUGUST 1813

Mr Edmund Kean, on two guineas a week, was the leading man of Mr Hughes's Company of Actors and Comedians at Exeter Theatre. His Harlequin was widely admired and the public lavished praise on his life and vigour, his amazing somersaulting as he dived through the traps in the scenery, his graceful dancing and, most of all, his vivacious vitality. But backstage was an embittered young man racked with pains from his exertions and physical torments caused by his excessive drinking. However, mental anguish caused him a greater agony. The public that flocked to admire his Harlequin stayed away from his Richard III, Othello and Hamlet. The man who originally proclaimed he would not support any actor other than John Philip Kemble had resorted to pleading for places in London in roles far humbler than the principal ones he was undertaking in Exeter and Weymouth and other theatres on Mr Hughes's circuit.

Mrs Kean, now a mother of two small children, realised that she had shackled herself to a less than rosy future. Her husband had degenerated from the shining leading man with a bright career ahead to a quarrelsome, poverty-stricken mountebank who drank away what little money they earned. Already she was heartily tired of the arguments with landladies, the absconding in the middle of the night because of debts, and her permanent battle against the ill-health of herself and her boys. But all her pleading was useless. Edmund was never at ease with himself; when he played Othello he complained of the ignorance of the audience. Lord Cork, reputed to be a connoisseur of the drama, on attending the play, paid no attention and spent the evening chuckling at the antics of his own children as they fooled around in his private box.

It was of no use Mary telling her husband he was the finest Harlequin for miles around and that he could make a good honest living in such roles in London.

The depths of Kean's misery were plumbed when the star actor Mr Betty came to visit. Mr Kean was seen by a friend, pacing up and down in anguish outside the theatre.

"He commands overflowing houses! I play to empty benches. I know my powers are far superior to his. He can't even speak properly! He is inaudible in the quiet parts, harsh and provincial in forceful moments."

Mr Kean's friend nodded sympathetically in agreement as Mr Kean went through a catalogue of Mr Betty's real and imagined failings. Being a friend of Mr Kean, he was unable to know if Edmund was superior to Mr Betty or not, but he thought to himself that surely not everybody could be wrong in flocking to Betty whilst ignoring Kean?

— They do say, Mr Betty, that genius is akin to madness.

— Did you know Cooke died in America?

— No.

— Well, when Kean went over there, because things were getting a bit hot for him here, he went to look for Cooke's grave. It was just an ordinary common grave so he got permission from the bishop there to erect a grand tomb and had the remains re-interred. He snaffled a toe bone and brought it home with him. When he arrived back, Elliston and the entire company from Drury Lane went out to Barnet to greet him and process back to the theatre with him. What do you think he made them do? He made each one in turn kneel down and kiss the hallowed toe bone. Can you imagine – this line of leading players all kissing a wretched bit of bone? Even Stephen Kemble had to do it and he was so fat he could play Falstaff without padding. They needed four men to lift him up again.

A very odd fellow, Kean. For some reason they had made him chief of a Red Indian tribe out there in the Wild West; so every now and then he would arrive at the theatre all tricked out in a feathered head-dress and war paint! The man was a raving lunatic!

— Yet he was a big star.

— And where is he now? Dead. Died at the same age I am now. Drunk himself into a pauper's grave. Here am I, robust and healthy – and rich. Now Kean's son is giving himself airs on our stages. Pushed on at Drury Lane at the age of sixteen as Young Norval. A complete stunt, of course. Failed dismally and he had to flee to the provinces. He spent two years in America and, now he is back they keep putting him up at Drury Lane to compete with Macready, but he is only trading on his father's reputation. I do not know why managers think the public should accept the son just because the father was popular! We seem to have drifted somewhat from our purpose. You are supposed to be making notes concerning *my* career, Mr Dickens.

— Sorry, sir. My most recent note says you had returned at your old money of fifty guineas a night, were the head of your profession and were hailed as the British Roscius.

— Ah, yes. Shortly after my return to the stage my dear little sister died. Gone before she could attain the age of ten years. The lease of the farm expired so I bought a cottage for my mother in the same area. I married and had a son —

— Wife's name?

— What? Is that important?

— I think your readers will be interested in personal details, Mr Betty.

— Do you think so? Susanna. Her father Joshua Crow was a near neighbour of ours. Mr Crow was quite a big landowner in those parts. I named my son William Henry after myself. He is my pride and joy. As he left infancy I decided that I should stay at home to oversee his upbringing. I had accumulated much wealth over my years of playing and I had no necessity to work. Thus, in spite of protestations from the public, who were always loyal to me, I decided to make my final bow from the stage. Just over ten years ago I gave my farewell performance and formally retired. And that is the end of my story.

— A life full of incident and excitement. Don't you find it rather dull now you're retired?

— Not at all. One changes as one gets older, Mr Dickens. I do not find it necessary to seek constant attention. I prefer a quiet life. Wealth helps a person to serenity. I thought your concluding paragraph might be something on these lines: "Our hero was now hailed as the English Roscius, a title that, with him, will be an evergreen, and shall grace his tomb with a never-fading wreath when the place that now knows him, shall know him no more." What do you think?

— If that's what you wish.

— Well I thought something on those lines would round it off rather nicely. Do you not think so?

— If that is what you wish. Do you prefer British Roscius or English Roscius? You have said both.

— Oh, I can adjust all that kind of thing when I check it through. Well that is basically my life story. Have you any questions?

— What's William Macready really like?

— I meant concerning my life!

— Oh, don't worry about that. I will make a good job of that for you. Especially if I can go through your press-cuttings book. It's only a matter of collecting together a lot of flattering comments from different people and sticking them all together with a few facts here and there. You'll be delighted with the result. Now tell me about Macready. You said you acted a lot with him.

— When we were both in our early twenties. Macready is a prig. He has starch up his arse instead of shit. He hates the theatre, you know. He despises his profession. He only went on the stage to save his father from bankruptcy. He wants to be a grand gentleman. That is why his acting is so insipid. He turns all his characters into gentlemen. You do not want a respectable Macbeth! An Othello with good manners! That is the trouble with the theatre today. Everybody is so worthy and dull. There are no characters any more.

Cooke was a huge star of the first magnitude. He was a character as large as the ones he played. When he gave his Richard at Liverpool with too much drink inside him and the audience started objecting, he marched straight down to the front and said "You dare to hiss me! Hiss George Frederick Cooke? You will not have the opportunity of hissing me again! *I* banish *you*! There is not a brick in your dirty town but what is cemented by the blood of a slave!" And stormed off. Wonderful character! In Sheffield he was doing Zanga, one of his most famous parts, when they started booing and he just stopped and said: "Cooke shall not appear before a pack of dirty knife-grinders!" and walked off.

— Surely he lost engagements with that behaviour?

— Oh, he would come back a couple of nights later, make a grovelling apology to the audience and they would cheer him to the echo. It was only the drink talking. When he was sober he was the most charming man in the world. Do anything for anybody. What a character!

— Are you still a friend of Mr Macready? I wonder if you could introduce me.

— Oh, I have not spoken to the man for years. He proved to be not as good a friend as his father had been. He still knows me, of course, but a man does not care to acknowledge a fellow he has wronged. I am still on the free list at both Drury Lane and Covent Garden. I do not often go. They are pygmies on the boards these days. We were giants!

— You don't admire Macready's playing?

— It is like watching myself! He has copied all my points. Uses all my business.

— But you call him dull.

— So he is. He has copied my actions and my speech but he cannot copy my genius. That is why he is dull. He is merely a studied actor with no inspiration or God-given naturalism. Pompous and aloof. Just stands there and declaims. Boring. We are in the nineteenth century now. We have gas lighting. We no longer go to hear a play, we go to see it. It is no longer sufficient merely to declaim. One has to act! I was taught that thirty years ago by – someone. Macready has not learned it yet. I tell you this: if I had not retired, Macready would not be where he is today. When we were young men I could act him off the stage and I could still do it today. But pray do not start me on that!

How long do you think it will take you to write up your notes in proper form?

— Is time of the essence?

— I would like it doing as soon as possible. You see, my son is to make his debut in six weeks' time and I would like to have this memoir all printed up ready for that.

— I see. You mean your son is about to go upon the stage?

— That is so. I have arranged for him to appear at the theatre in Gravesend. He is to make his debut as Selim in *Barbarossa*. The same part with which I dazzled London all those years ago.

— How old is your son?

— Henry is fifteen.

— So we shall see Master Betty II?

— There will never be another Master Betty. I have purposely delayed his debut until he is of a more mature age. I have been instructing him in my range of parts since he was ten years old. I do not wish to launch him as an infant prodigy but as a proper actor. I have waited until his voice broke and his nutmegs dropped. My plan is to try him out quietly in a few country theatres to build up his confidence and test his ability. Of which I have not the slightest doubt. Henry will be a fine actor, nay more, I foresee a glittering future for him. How can it be otherwise with my experience and knowledge? With Betty blood flowing through his veins? After a couple of years I will then place him in larger theatres in the principal towns before making an assault on the capital itself.

— So you have it all planned?

— Like a military campaign. It has been done before. I have learned something from my Friends.

— Then you'll require my work as soon as possible if you are to hand it to a printer and have it published in six weeks' time.

— Yes, I hope I have not delayed too long in mounting this enterprise. I have a printer waiting who assures me he will be able to commence immediately he receives my manuscript.

— You said you required only a short work?

— Yes, perhaps only three-dozen pages. I would like to be able to sell it for no more than a shilling. I intend it to be available at the theatres where Henry plays.

— I have to go to Kettering and Northampton on business, but you shall have it within the week.

— Goodness, you do get about, Mr Dickens.

— By-elections, Mr Betty.

— Of course. Hogarth told me you were parliamentary correspondent for the *Morning Chronicle*.

1834

Mrs Dickens had a wide circle of friends and relations, and she was not reticent about approaching them for assistance. It was less embarrassing to ask for work for her son than to have her husband pestering them for money handouts. Thus, Charles's uncle came to his aid with a more interesting position where his professional talents could be used; that of parliamentary reporter on his paper *Mirror of Parliament*.

It is a fortunate man who enjoys his work. Many men find that, at some period in their maturity, they look at themselves and realise that they have spent many years doing work that they had somehow drifted into in their youth, that years have swiftly passed by without their realising it and what had at the time seemed to be but a temporary step on their ladder of ambition had in actuality become a platform where they remained for the rest of their life. Some men found themselves in an occupation that was not too uncongenial and were content with their life. Others, who were less fortunate, found that they had been obliged to work in unrewarding occupations simply to keep their families fed and clothed and away from penury. At the end of their lives such men must have wondered what the purpose of it all was. But neither is it sufficient for a man to be ambitious if he has not the knowledge or skill necessary to pursue his dreams. It is no good aspiring to be a juggler if you are hopeless at catching balls.

Charles found himself in the happy position of a man who enjoyed his work. His life had once again been influenced by one of his many relatives. His uncle's new publication *Mirror of Parliament* was devoted to printing all the proceedings of

Parliament. He conceived it as a rival to *Hansard* the long-established publisher of those matters. It is not clear why he thought such a publication be necessary as the whole point was to record as accurately as possible the speeches given in the two houses. We can thus dismiss the thought of political bias towards one party. Knowing that his nephew, after four years of labouring at Doctors' Commons, was a skilled shorthand practitioner, he offered him a post on his new publication. It was an exciting time to be in politics as a revolution was taking place in 1832. A change in the country was in the air – less bloody than the one a generation or two ago in France, but just as profound for the future of the nation. For six months Charles had also written pieces for the radical newspaper *True Sun* and flirted with the idea of seeking fame in the political sphere. However, his sentiments did not always chime with the policies of either of the leading parties and he preferred to view politics with some impartiality.

As well as being satisfied with his work, Charles was very content with his private life. His amateur dramatic activities provided great fun to all the young people of his family and their friends, as well as serving as an outlet for his mimicry. His love of the theatre saw him attending as many entertainments as he could afford and cram into his week.

The disadvantage in working for his uncle was that when Parliament had risen he was without work and without pay. In the 1833 recess he wrote to the private secretary of Lord Stanley, whom he knew had praised the accuracy and quality of his work, to see if he had anything for the summer months. But, alas, whilst reiterating his master's praise he regretted he had nothing to offer.

Thus it was that, to fill his spare time, Charles started writing articles and slight, amusing descriptions of London life. These he submitted to various newspapers under the pseudonym of Boz which he hoped would indicate the comic aspects of his sketches. The invention of the steam press had made printing a much cheaper process and, whereas in Sir Walter Scott's time a three-volume novel had to be priced at thirty shillings, now novels were being produced in one volume at six shillings. There were daily newspapers both morning and evening, weekly papers, monthly magazines and quarterly journals at all prices – with contents aimed at different classes and intellects. A poor man who could read was no longer debarred by cost; he could buy a monthly magazine for sixpence and a newspaper for a penny. The population of London was increasing rapidly and new newspapers and magazines were springing up almost daily to cater for the clustered proletariat.

Charles's first success was the publication of one his sketches *A Dinner at Poplar Walk* in the *Monthly Magazine* (price 2/6d, circulation 1000) for which he was paid nothing. But there are few things more satisfying in life than seeing one's work in print, to be read by strangers who pay for the privilege. A man feels that what he has to say is of value to other people and he is not just a loud-mouthed bore trying to impress. Dickens found that editors liked his pieces which were essentially frivolous but based on the true characters that he observed all around him in his daily life. Without realising it he had transformed his talent for mimicry into print.

Three daily serious newspapers – the *Morning Chronicle*, the *Times* and the *Morning Herald* – were respected for their parliamentary reports and each employed a team of a dozen shorthand reporters. Each man did a forty-five minute shift before dashing back to his office to transcribe his scribblings, giving way to a colleague to continue. A relay race of words. Charles sat amongst these men squashed into the public gallery and soon gained a reputation as being one of the best. His quality came to the attention of the *Morning Chronicle* editor who took him on at five guineas a week. Although in this position Charles did nothing different from the duties he had previously been doing for his uncle on the *Mirror of Parliament*, there was no lay-off in the summer recess and his new post included reporting other matters. He was sent to Edinburgh to report on a dinner for Earl Grey, Devon to cover the hustings, Bristol, Northamptonshire. It was arduous work but Charles thrived on hard work if he thought it worthwhile. This was a life he understood. Taking shorthand notes, travelling by post-chaise through the night, transcribing his notes by flickering light as he went, arriving at his office to write up the piece for the compositors and relaxing exhausted as his words winged out into the waiting world. He was, at last, doing an important job. He was a parliamentary correspondent. He was doing something to serve his fellow men.

— I will tell you something of great interest about Parliament. When I made my debut as Hamlet at Covent Garden, Mr Pitt the prime minister adjourned Parliament so that the members could all come to see me play. There! That is the impression I caused in London. It would be a good story to include in the memoir.

— I will put it in.

— Before you go, permit me to give you some fatherly advice – or rather, as you have a living father, shall we say avuncular advice, Mr Dickens. Do not become over-inflated with a sense of your own importance.

— You said I may take your album of press-cuttings?

— Of course, of course. Here, wrap it in this paper. I must caution you to guard that very carefully, Mr Dickens; that parcel contains a man's life.

— Not all of it, Mr Betty, not all of it. Good day.

— Allow me to see you to the door. Here is your very smart hat and cane. Goodbye, Mr Dickens.

Mr Betty escorts his visitor to the door and watches as his amanuensis swaggers down the road with Mr Betty's precious album tucked under his arm. Mr Betty is left alone once more. He stands by the window pondering. He wonders whether this bumptious youth is the right man for the job. He speaks his next thought out loud: "Next time I give the man a shilling to clean out the privy I will regard it as a business partnership!"

Part Two
1836

Mr Dickens

CHARLES DICKENS alights from his cab at the corner of the square and strides purposefully across towards Mr Betty's house. After a childhood of many vicissitudes, it is very pleasant to be twenty-five years of age, in regular employment, in love and engaged to be married. It is even more pleasant to be offered a better job with better pay and prospects at the same time. If, alongside this, you are free-lancing as a successful author you are in seventh heaven. This is the fortunate position in which Mr Charles Dickens now finds himself. The previous evening he had jotted down on a piece of paper his current station in life:

Item   Position with the *Morning Chronicle* and *Evening Chronicle*.
        7 guineas weekly.
Item   Collection of *Sketches by Boz* published by Mr Macrone. £100.
Item   Series *Pickwick* to be published in monthly parts by Chapman & Hall. 9 guineas per month.
Item   Burletta *The Village Coquettes* with Mr Hullah to be staged December. Value ?
Item   Farce *The Strange Gentleman* to be staged September. Value ?
Item   Novel *Gabriel Vardon* for Mr Macrone. £200 advance.
Item   Children's Book *Solomon Bell the Raree Showman* for Mr Tegg. £100 advance.
Item   Two full-length novels for Mr Bentley. £500 each.
Item   Series of Sketches for the *Carlton Chronicle*. 5 guineas weekly.
Item   New collection of Sketches for Mr Macrone. £100.
Item   *Memoir of Joseph Grimaldi*. Value ?
Item   Editorship of *Bentley's Miscellany* on offer. NB would have to resign from *MC* & *EC*.

Not at all bad, he thinks, for a man to achieve in little more than a year. It is well-known that there is a thing called overnight success but it is not usually realised that the so-called 'overnight' has often been an accumulation of hard work and the striving of many years. Sometimes an overnight success elides into a nine days' wonder. Dickens is determined not to slip back into obscurity and penury ever again. He is a strong man and cannot see why once advantage has been gained it should ever be relinquished.

Dickens is on the way to a dinner engagement and is dressed elegantly in the latest most fashionable manner. He has recently acquired a black woollen cloak with blue lining that he wears thrown back over the shoulder in the Spanish manner. In the fifteen months since we last saw him Dickens has bloomed. He is a much more confident and self-assured man with an air of success about him. His dinner engagement is not until two hours hence but, realising that his hostess lives not very far from his erstwhile employer, he has set off early so that he can detour to have a few words with Mr Betty whom he has not seen since the encounter previously described.

Dickens, as he swaggers along the road, considers he has some unfinished business to which he must attend. As he arrives at Mr Betty's house on the corner of Ampthill Square he is surprised to see the man himself inside the wide open door, on his hands and knees.

— Good afternoon, Mr Betty. What can you be doing?

— Dropped my blessed key.

— Why, here it is on the step!

— Outside? How did it get there? I am sure I dropped it in here.

— Perhaps it bounced?

— Well thank you kindly, sir. Good heavens, it is the shorthand writer!

— Dickens, sir; how do you do?

— How do you do, it is good to see you again. Come you in, come you in.

— I hope I'm not intruding? I'm promised for dinner at Miss Burdett Coutts. Her house is not far from you so I thought I would set off early in the hope of finding you at home.

— Miss Burdett Coutts, eh? She is the richest heiress in all England.

— So I believe.

— I had just slipped out for a couple of bottles then dropped the door key getting back in. I am leading a bachelor existence at present. Mrs Betty is on her annual visit to the country. She always takes a couple of months in Shropshire at this time of year. Visits her old friends.

— I didn't have the pleasure of meeting Mrs Betty on my previous visit.

— No. She is not much interested in theatrical affairs. She likes country pursuits but they bore me to tears. I am a city man, myself. I like a bit of bustle about me. I have tried the country and found it dull. So she makes an annual pilgrimage back home to do her round of visits. It suits me. It suits.

— And how are you, Mr Betty?

— Oh, quite happy, quite happy. I drink too much, of course. That is probably why I am happy, eh? And yourself? It must be several months since our interview?

— Over a year in fact, sir.

— Is it really? You astonish me. Good gracious me, how time flies. *Tempus fugit,* eh?

— I hope I don't inconvenience you. I'm sorry for dropping in on you unexpectedly but I wanted to apologise and, at the same time, thank you.

— Apologise?

— Yes. It was remiss of me to keep your press-cuttings book for so long.

— Ah, that. It was rather lax of you, sir, especially after I had said how much I valued it. When I received your manuscript so promptly I could not believe that I would be under the necessity of hounding you for the return of my own property.

— I'd to work quickly to get your memoir finished within the promised week but your story so fascinated me that I wished to savour it. I'm afraid I kept your book longer than was proper. I hope I'm forgiven?

— Your letter of apology was most handsomely written. I forgave you the minute the album was returned. Pray think no more of it.

— You're very kind. I also wished to thank you. Because of my work for you I've received a similar commission. I've been asked to write the memoirs of Mr Grimaldi the well-known clown.

— Old Joey? Good Lord. I did not realise he was still alive.

— He's very frail. Although not yet sixty.

— I have not heard of old Joey for years. But then I suppose they say the same about me!

— He's been retired these fifteen years.

— Not much longer than me.

— Unlike you, sir, Joey's retirement was enforced. The poor man had to give up his work; his legs had gone. The result of a lifetime leaping and tumbling for our amusement. I'm afraid his declining years have not been too happy. Did you know his son?

— No. I never mixed with pantomime performers.

— His son turned out a bit of a ne'er-do-well. He caused his father great grief. Got into debt, became a drunkard. He died three or four years ago. Then last year Joey's wife died so he's all on his own.

— Very sad. He was so popular in his day. He must have earned a lot of money.

— The troubles with his son cost him dearly and, after fifteen years of retirement, his savings are virtually gone. I was with him the other night. He's trying to sell his musical instruments and theatrical properties. He has little else of value.

— Unfortunately we are all at the whims of ageing and ill-health.

— His body is totally arthritic and his legs will not support him at all. It's all due to the exertions of his youth. I suggested he call his memoirs *Crippled by Clowning* but he wouldn't hear of it. He retains his sense of the humorous grotesque. He's developed a system: kind friends take him by cart to his local tavern and at closing time the landlord gives him a piggy-back home. Did you ever appear together on the stage?

— Good Lord no! Joey was a pantomimist. He only appeared in the afterpieces. Mind you, I loved to watch the Harlequinade from the wings. Most fascinating. The scene has several flaps and traps and the performers chase each other and dive through the scenery. It is quite a dangerous proceeding because they rely on stagehands holding canvas sheets to catch them on the other side. Those men are not reliable. If they are not given a good tip or if they take against a certain artiste they may not be there to catch him. Oh, it can be a grievous business, the Harlequinade.

— Well thanks to somebody reading your memoirs I've been asked to do a full length Life of Mr Grimaldi. And how are sales of your memoirs? I thought I made a decent job of them.

— To be honest, Mr Dickens, they do not sell at all. We sold some copies at my son's debut. That was the idea of course, to introduce him as the son of the Young Roscius. And as that personage has not been heard of for nigh on thirty years it was necessary to remind the public. No, the main purpose was to distribute my story to a chosen band of people that would be of assistance to my son's career. Theatre managers, newspaper editors and other influential persons. Although we sold quite a few copies to the public at the theatre at Gravesend.

— I was sorry I couldn't get to your son's debut. How did things go?

— Oh, wonderfully well. Not a completely full house but an appreciative one.

— I suppose he's touring all over the country now?

— No, Henry is studying at a theological college.

— Really? How surprising. So you may have a clergyman for a son rather than an actor?

— Quite possibly.

— Although they do say that the two professions are almost indistinguishable.

— What? Eh, oh, ha, very good.

— Then his plans fall in with your wishes?

— Most certainly. I do not believe in imposing my will. He shall be his own master. When he comes of age. He is sixteen, no, he must be turned seventeen by now – Good Lord! Mind you I think he will become an actor.

— You do?

— Definitely. There is nothing like it. I often think I should have stayed with it. I am only forty-six now, you know. Plenty of life in me still. But the next generation beckons, eh? Henry has the genius. How could it be otherwise, being my son? It would be a great loss to the world if he does not tread the boards. After all he does have the blood of Young Roscius coursing through his veins. I shall not live for ever and once I have gone Master Betty could well be forgotten.

— I'm afraid that is the fate of most of us. Man's ever present desire – to be remembered.

— I thought it my duty to place the facts in print so that our descendents would know the true story of Master Betty the Young Roscius and what he meant to the people of his time. Now through your work, although the author will never be renowned, Master Betty will be immortal. But tell me, Mr Dickens, what have you been up to since our last meeting?

— Actually, sir, I've had some exceptionally good fortune. For some time now I've contributed pieces to various magazines and newspapers and a collection of them is about to be published in the form of a book.

— A book eh? Excellent, excellent. I shall look out for it and shall certainly purchase a copy. What is the title?

— *Sketches by Boz. Illustrative of Every Day Life and Every Day People*. Boz is my *nom-de-plume*. I've also been commissioned to write a comic novel in twenty monthly parts.

— Excellent indeed! Mr Hogarth said you were an up-and-coming young man. Well you do sound to have much work on your hands. All that and Grimaldi too.

— I'm the kind of man who is not happy being idle.

— Ah, there we differ. I am the kind of man who is. And as I have sufficient wealth I am able to indulge my whim.

— Since I last saw you my work has taken me to Edinburgh, reporting on Lord Grey. I've also covered the Suffolk elections at Ipswich and Sudbury. In fact I've been rattling around the country much as you must have done in your touring days. I'm also to marry very soon.

— Hogarth's girl?

— Miss Catherine Hogarth, the eldest daughter of our mutual friend.

— I hope you are suitably matched and wish you much joy.

— Thank you. As well as all that I've also undertaken much private research.

— Really? Your prodigious capacity quite exhausts me. In what branch of science do you research?

— The human soul.

— Good gracious me! That sounds a very onerous and daunting task.

— To be more exact I should say one person's soul.

— One person's soul! That is most curious. May I ask who this person is?

— You, sir.

— Me? You astonish me, Dickens. Why should my soul be of interest to you?

— All men's souls are of interest to me. I'm a writer. My encounter with you, Mr Betty, has intrigued me very much. You see, your youth was so very different from mine that I was eager to learn more.

— More, sir? I related to you the story of my life. What more has a man to offer?

— The truth.

— The truth? What do you mean by that, sir? Are you accusing me of telling you lies?

— No, Mr Betty, I don't say that. But interesting as your story was – is, I think there is much more that you did not reveal to me.

— What else is there to reveal? I told you my life. You wrote it up in an acceptable form for the world to read. That is the end of it. One contented subject, one author richer by twenty-five guineas and an entertaining read for an idle hour. What more can anyone want? That is, after all, the prime purpose of literature.

— I found it remarkable that, having been such a centre of attraction in your extreme youth, as a man you could give it all up and live quietly and humbly without any regrets.

— That is not so very remarkable. I am assured in my present position in the world. I have no need to dwell on the past. I am well content with the present. I am not such a shallow creature that I must forever lust for worldly fame. If I were old and broken like Joe Grimaldi then I might be embittered. But I have a living wife and a dutiful son. I have also accumulated great wealth which is always a comfort.

— I was particularly curious about something specific you said in your most interesting narrative. You said that when you performed Hamlet for the first time at Drury Lane the prime minister Mr Pitt adjourned Parliament so that its members could see you act.

— Well?

— That is not true.

— What do you mean not true? What do you mean, sir? Pitt was there, Fox was there, Canning was there. They were all there – all the blessed government, and opposition too!

— I'm sure they were. I don't dispute those men were present at your debut as Hamlet. Indeed your newspaper cuttings mention their presence in particular.

— Well then.

— They didn't have to adjourn Parliament to be there. You acted Hamlet for the first time at Drury Lane on 14th March 1805. Parliament wasn't sitting that night.

— Not sitting? I do not follow you, sir.

— On that night the members were not sitting so were free to attend your performance.

— Oh, I am sure you are mistaken. I have been told the story ever since that night. It is a proud family legend.

— Legend is all it is. It never happened.

— You are mistaken, sir.

— No, sir. I am a parliamentary shorthand writer. I'm fully conversant with the ways of Parliament. I've full access to the library of reports housed there. I've gone through the entire sittings of Parliament held during your seasons at Drury Lane and Covent Garden in 1804/5 and 1805/6 and there is no mention of an adjournment for the members to visit the theatre to see you as Hamlet – or any other role. I'm sorry.

— Well, I am dumbfounded. There must have been some mistake. I was surely told that fact on the night. I was told it then and several times afterwards. Indeed my father made mention of it more than once when writing to theatre managers.

— I'm sure he did. Your father was an astute promoter.

— But they were there – Pitt, Fox, Canning and the rest. They were there.

— Certainly they were there. That night and on other occasions.

— And Mr Fox did say that my Hamlet surpassed John Philip Kemble's!

— He's reported as saying that.

— Well then. That is what really matters.

— While Pitt didn't adjourn a sitting to come and see you play, I do wonder if he conspired with Fox to boost you.

— What do you mean "boost" me?

— They could see how all fashionable London was besotted with Master Betty, realising too that he was a great distraction from the French War. Perhaps they decided it was in both their parties' interests to keep the frenzy going. Napoleon's army of invasion was poised to attack at any time and we were ill-prepared. A distraction was very opportune.

MARCH 1805

The debate in Parliament had been fierce and angry, much vapid air and haughty words being expended to very little result. The problem was that nobody had realised that Napoleon's plans were so advanced. There was now no doubt at all that Napoleon Buonaparte was massing his forces along the Channel coast from Antwerp to Brest in readiness to invade Britain. The nation was in peril and completely unprepared. William Pitt the prime minister had urged George III to summon a coalition government as the best way to combat the invader but he was totally opposed to the inclusion of Charles James Fox – probably the most able politician of the day. So debates tended to become a matter of Fox opposing every proposal of Pitt and vice versa. In their younger days the two had been friends but a bitter dispute some twenty years previously had turned them into rancorous enemies. Pitt often thought he was not only expected to fight Napoleon but Fox as well.

Now things were looking very bad indeed. Methods of defence were urgently sought. Intelligence reports told of two thousand craft already in harbour ready to attack and a hundred and fifty thousand armed men assembled ready to leave. A suggestion that the Dungeness peninsula should be flooded by opening the sluice gates and breaking the banks of the Rivers Rother and Brede had been rejected back in May as impractical but by September eagerly adopted. In August the Duke of York had suggested building a line of defence towers and these were already under construction with, to date, some eighty-six of them in place. A military canal was also being dug with the dual purpose of being a barrier to the enemy and a means of moving supplies to the forces. Platoons of soldiers were being deployed along the south coast, but the coast of southern Britain is long and no intelligence told of where Napoleon would launch his attack. There was no doubt that the British navy was the finest in the world and many MPs were complacent, thinking that any invasion by sea would be easily countered. Once the French army was on land then it would be a very different matter. The proposed strategy would have to be a tactical withdrawal of forces back towards the capital, taking up defensive positions on the North Downs to protect London. It was heavily rumoured that Napoleon was ready, waiting for the first foggy night in which to launch his attack. An entire army could cross the Channel in a handful of hours.

Leaving the Palace of Westminster the prime minister was surprised to be accosted by Fox.

"Can I give you a lift home in my carriage, Mr Pitt, or are you bound for your club?"

"I am going straight home and my own carriage awaits," replied Pitt stiffly.

"Then be so kind as to dismiss it and permit me to take you home. I have a good reason to request this."

As the carriage bumped along the cobbles Fox said "Have you been to see this new boy actor Master Betty?"

"No, I do not frequent the theatre at the present time. I have too many demands."

"He is causing quite a furore. The newspapers are full of him."

"I have noticed."

"I went to see him last night."

"Is he any good?"

"A pleasant enough youth. He remembered all his lines, walked on and off without bumping into anything. Clear diction, graceful deportment which seems to please the ladies. Other than that – commonplace."

"You have asked to accompany me merely to discuss a commonplace youth?"

"There are rumblings that we are ill-prepared to repel

Napoleon. The newspapers are criticising you daily. Even the common people fear the invasion is imminent."

"People always criticise the government, and you – the leader of the Opposition – have criticised every plan the government has made. Do not seek a coalition. I have tried to persuade the King of it but he is your implacable enemy, he does not want you in any position of power."

"Tut, tut, I know all that. It is not of that which I speak. It is not of advantage to any of us that Parliament looks weak and ill-prepared. You know as well as I that if Napoleon lands all is lost."

"We will stop him at sea."

"Our country is isolated. All our enemies have either been defeated or made peace with Buonaparte. I have intelligence that Spain proposes an alliance with him, against us."

"Have you placed me in your carriage to frighten me? I am not a child who is made to eat his dinner by his nurse saying if he does not then Boney will get him."

"At the moment everybody is besotted with Master Betty but he is a bubble and no doubt soon this bubble will burst. It is, however, in all our interests that we keep it afloat. If society is reading about Master Betty, watching Master Betty, their minds are taken off Buonaparte. The daily papers are full of this child, important news is buried inside the back pages. This is greatly to be encouraged."

"You want all our citizens to fawn over this jumped-up mountebank while the country goes to hell in a handcart?"

"You put it so well, Mr Pitt. Exactly that. If we can keep the bubble going until Napoleon is defeated, the nation will never know how near it was to disaster."

"But what can Parliament do? Society chooses its own favourites to lionise. For instance, I know you are more highly regarded than I am. On what trivial grounds I could not say."

"I am not speaking of Parliament, Mr Pitt. I am speaking of government. You and I both know that it is possible to influence by subtle means."

"Underhand , you mean."

"Certainly. There are leaders in society, not always men of probity, who seem to be able to sway the great and the good. People like George Brummell."

"Pah! Useless popinjay who leads the Prince of Wales astray."

"Just so. People are followers of fashion and, at the moment, Master Betty is the height of fashion. Believe me, we must keep him so. You and I, with Canning and one or two prominent others, must attend one of his performances. If it is seen that we are relaxed and enjoying ourselves like society folk the word will spread. Our statesmen are not afraid of any old Buonaparte. Let him huff and puff across the Channel. Remember the story of Sir Francis Drake who insisted on finishing his game of bowls before he gave a thought to defeating the Spanish armada. That should be our attitude."

Pitt silently cogitated a while. "Perhaps you are right. Anything to avoid these press hacks criticising us."

"Master Betty gives his Hamlet on Thursday. Are you free?"

"I will make it my business to be so."

"Good. I will arrange for seats."

"Separate boxes."

"Of course."

The prime minister, stepping down from the carriage without a further word, entered his house going straight to dinner where his niece awaited him.

The *Morning Post* of 15th March reported many leading politicians were present for Master Betty's Hamlet and applauded him to the echo. Mr Fox was quoted as saying he considered Master Betty to be superior to Garrick and that the boy was a true ornament of the stage. The news that the French Admiral Villeneuve had managed to evade Nelson's blockade of Toulon harbour and was heading for the West Indies, with Nelson in pursuit, was relegated to an inside page.

— Your wild theory that members of Parliament praised my performances merely to distract the public from the threat of invasion is an insult to me, sir. And to the memory of my friends. Where on earth have you got this preposterous idea?

— I've said that I'm well-versed in the ways of Parliament. There are men there who remember very well the furore you caused. They called it Bettymania and say what a useful purpose it served.

— Where is your proof of this? Not even my severest critics have ever made such an outrageous suggestion.

— There is no proof. The ways of government are devious. There are many things that happen in the nation's interest that nobody ever learns about. It's not always wise to put pen to paper.

— This is just ancient gossip you have picked up from embittered old hacks!

— I don't think so. As you, yourself, told me – on the morning that it was reported that Napoleon had been crowned emperor, the newspapers spread Master Betty all over the pages while giving Napoleon a mere paragraph.

— I do not believe a word of this!

— That's your prerogative. I only offer the suggestion.

— You appear to be allying yourself with that sector of the press who delighted in holding me up to ridicule. Mr Leigh Hunt and all his scurrilous friends.

— No, sir. I do not ridicule you at all. The frenzy you caused is a true phenomenon. I'm nonplussed at this distance of time to account for it. I can't see it happening in the present day. I can't imagine the fashionable world becoming so besotted with one young person nowadays. To crowd outside your hotel for a mere glimpse! Articles in the papers setting out your weight and dimensions! Pinning facsimiles on their walls! I think mania is truly the word.

— That is because I was a Gift from God. Such men are very rare.

— You tell us the highest in the land invited you to their houses. Ladies of quality petted you and tried to kiss you.

— They did, they did.

— You must have been an extraordinary boy.

— I was a graceful and beautiful youth. I know that is hard to believe now. But in those days I had a head of golden ringlets and a smile that melted the hearts of half London. I was hailed as a National Treasure!

— So can you be surprised that I wanted to learn all I could about you?

— But I am here, sir. I live and breathe. Thirty years older but still the same person. I can tell you everything you wish to know. You do not have to grub about in parliamentary libraries!

— But sir, as we have seen, you can be mistaken.

— Mistaken, sir?

— Perhaps misinformed?

— That incident which you have seized upon is a mere bagatelle. So Parliament was not adjourned. Still they came.

— They did. But the adjournment of Parliament is part of your legend.

— You must understand, Mr Dickens, that I was a mere boy when all this happened. I was either acting, travelling, meeting important people or eating and sleeping. It is like a dream to me now. I look back as though it happened to another person. But it was me. My youth. It is all still in my head and heart.

— You said that you were born at your mother's estate at Hopton Wafers, near Shrewsbury.

— That is correct. Even you, Dickens, are surely not about to dispute where I was born!

— Of course not. I just wondered why you left there to go to Ireland when you were five years old.

— I really cannot assist you. A five-year-old boy is not privy to his parents' actions or the reasons for them. I have no idea.

— Perhaps your father got into financial difficulties and your mother's estate had to be sold to enable him to extricate himself?

— That is an outrageous suggestion, sir!

— I merely offer it as a possibility. When I was a boy of twelve my father got himself into financial trouble and was imprisoned in the Marshalsea. You will not be acquainted with the debtors' prison, Mr Betty. It is a place to be avoided. Unfortunately if one has a tendency to live beyond one's means it is an ever-present danger. My father was confined for some time and I was sent to scrape a pathetic living at Warren's Blacking factory at Hungerford Stairs.

FEBRUARY 1824

Charles was as wretched and miserable as he had ever been in his short life. Two days after his twelfth birthday he was sent to Warren's Blacking factory near Hungerford Bridge. His mother had presented this to him as a great opportunity. She had prevailed on distant family connections in the figure of the owner of this upstart company which was not the famous Warren's Blacking Company but a lesser enterprise trying to trade on the greater's reputation. Mr James Lamert, the son of his old theatre-going companion in Chatham, had agreed to take Charles on at six shillings a week to do general office work and, in the lunch hour, to instruct him in matters of commerce.

The reality of his situation turned out to have been somewhat inflated and he found every day a period of misery and torture. He rose at first light in the garret room he shared with another child in Camden – a desolate place amongst fields and ditches – breakfasted on a penny loaf and a penn'orth of milk then walked the three miles down through the centre of London, across the Strand to Hungerford Stairs on the Thames. His place of work was a rotting wooden warehouse with collapsing floors and stairs which lurched over the very water; his workday accompanied by the noisome activity of the river and the scamperings of rats in the fetid scantlings.

The fiction of training was soon abandoned. Charles found himself no more than a mindless drudge whose job was to take small pots filled with boot blacking, add a greaseproof paper cover, trim with scissors and then tie with string. When he had done a gross of them he then had to paste printed labels on each one before they were despatched he knew not where, for sale to the public. He felt his situation very keenly. His father was not a gentleman but he was a respectable man, a clerk who had worked for the navy with postings at Portsmouth, Sheerness and Chatham as well as Somerset House in Town. This good man, whilst maintaining that education was the key to a man's upward progression, was denying his eldest son that very thing. His sister's good fortune affected Charles acutely. He brooded on how his own promising education had been savagely curtailed and why he had been sent to do menial work amongst low common men and boys from the lowest classes. The shame and humiliation he felt made him weep as he had been encouraged by his parents to think of himself as a boy of infinite promise with a future in some respectable profession such as the law. He had visions of, perhaps, becoming a great man – a man who was regarded and respected by similar great men. These visions were now dashed, crushed, and despair, desolation and degradation took their place. Inwardly he railed both against his mother, who had so cheerfully condemned him to this miserable existence, and his father who was so improvident. He railed against God for deserting him.

His long day over, he would trudge back, via St Martin's Lane and Tottenham Court Road, to his garret where he supped off another penny loaf and a quarter pound of cheese before crawling into his bed unloved, unwanted and unregarded.

Charles could not remember how long he had suffered at the blacking factory. He felt he had endured a whole lifetime. Each day his young heart sank as he dragged himself towards his place of work. There was no respite. Only on Sundays was he able to forget his work. On Sundays he and his sister Fanny would visit the rest of the family in the Marshalsea where Mr Dickens beamed on his brood like any proud father. To Charles these visits were like twisting a knife in his guts. The rest of his family were together and – although incarcerated – protected, housed and fed. His sister was a privileged person boarding amongst other young ladies of musical aptitude and receiving a sound and practical education, whilst he was nothing but a common labourer toiling twelve hours a day doing menial tasks amongst low common people.

Either Mr Lamert was making good profits, or his building was becoming too ramshackle to occupy, because he moved his enterprise to new premises in Chandos Street near to Covent Garden. Charles had acquired great dexterity in his menial task and, together with another boy called Bob Fagin, sat in the window of the new premises where their repetitious work became a minor attraction with passers-by stopping to admire their skill. One day his father, who had gained release from the Marshalsea by the providential bequest of a small sum from his mother's will, passed by and saw his son at work.

Mr Dickens had a great argument with Mr Lamert, resulting in Charles being taken away. His father assured him that no more would he suffer the degradation of sitting in a public window doing base chores. He professed he had not known the sort of work his son was doing and had understood from Mrs Dickens that Charles was a clerk being instructed in commercial matters. Charles was naturally overjoyed but, when the pair returned home, his mother was outraged that her husband had rowed with her kind relative who had done so much for their son. She insisted that Mr Dickens go back and make his peace. It is never pleasant for a child to hear his parents having a shouting match, especially when he is the subject of the dispute and Charles, putting his hands over his ears, shrank into a corner in an attempt to make himself invisible. He was appalled that his mother wanted to send him back. Back to that awful place of dirt, murk and misery. She did not succeed as his father prevailed, but for the rest of his life Charles never forgave his mother.

— Even when my father was released my mother wanted me to go back to that awful place. I'll never forgive her for that as long as I live. I swore an oath that I would better myself and never return to such degradation. Your story made me envious. I, sold into virtual slavery, while you at a similar age were idolised, lionised and rewarded with gold in extravagant quantity.

— You cannot compare yourself with Master Betty, Dickens. He was not as other mortals. He was a Child of Nature, a Gift from God.

— When you first went on the stage at Belfast, how old were you?

— I was just about to turn thirteen years old.

— And you were immediately greeted with rapture and acclaim?

— Indeed I was. Surely you read all about that in my cuttings album? You retained possession of it long enough.

— I noted that in your album there were significant gaps. Spaces where cuttings had obviously been glued in and then removed.

— I know nothing of that. My mother compiled the album. It is her work. That is how it was passed to me.

— I read your album most carefully. I read and marvelled.

— It is a marvellous tale it tells.

— I marvelled that, if you were such a success, you were not retained for further performances.

— What do you mean?

— I would have thought the manager at Belfast would have done his uttermost to keep such an outstanding attraction at his theatre.

— I could not stay. I was booked to go on to Dublin where I repeated my success.

— I think not. After your debut at Belfast you had a space of several weeks before your season at Dublin. There was ample opportunity for you to perform for a few extra nights then, or return some weeks later, to capitalise on your triumph.

— Then I should imagine that the Belfast theatre had other attractions already booked. I really do not know, Mr Dickens. I was a boy. I had no inkling of the arrangements made for my appearances. I was taken to where I was to appear. Told my role in the morning, rehearsed with the company and that night on I went. I did not concern myself with the bookings and negotiations with managers. My Friends did all that.

— In Dublin the newspaper reports say you acted to enormous acclaim. In fact the reports give praise in almost identical words to the Belfast papers. But again you passed on. No further performances. No return bookings.

— Again I repeat – all that had nothing to do with me.

— So on you went to Wexford and Waterford and the other principal cities of Ireland. At each you played your parts and in each town the newspapers lauded you to the skies.

— That is so.

— In terms so analogous it almost suggests the reports are by the same hand.

— You have all the evidence in my press-cuttings album.

— I found it very interesting that, although you were in Ireland, short items concerning you began to appear in the London press.

— What is strange in that? A phenomenon is a phenomenon wherever it takes place and is of interest to the whole world.

— I'm also intrigued by the way the newspapers referred to your advisers. 'Master Betty's Friends' was the usual mode.

— What is peculiar about that?

— I merely wondered who these Friends were. You say that your contracts were managed by your father. Was your mother classed as one of your Friends?

— I do not understand what you mean.

— Well, obviously your father was paramount in obtaining engagements, negotiating your fees and so on. I wondered if your mother had a part in your career. Perhaps she assisted with your elocution or designed your costumes?

— Shortly prior to my London debut my mother gave birth to my beloved only sister, God rest her soul. I rather think she had more on her hands than teaching me elocution or constructing costumes!

— But she no doubt luxuriated in the position of mother to the Young Roscius?

— Mr Dickens, I will speak plainly to you since you seem so earnestly to desire it. My mother had no part in my extraordinary career. She did not even approve of it. She called it my vagabondage. It was her greatest wish to see me leave the stage and go to university. Which I did, to please her. She was a sincere, good, honest woman who wanted the best for her son. She did not think it was good for my health to racket around the countryside performing in theatres every night. But she was a dutiful wife. My father brought great wealth into our family by his shrewd management of my career. She was heartbroken when he died. Her only consolation being the wealth he had created enabling her to live peacefully and comfortably as long as she may be spared.

— There appear to be some anomalies in your story.

— Anomalies? So? What is that to you? You have done your work.

— I have, and followed your instructions faithfully. If I'd been writing for myself, however, there are several questions that would give me pause.

— Well you were not writing for yourself. Unless –. You are not one of these gutter-raking journalists? Parasites who trawl through people's lives looking for some hidden scandal. Are you a mere Grub Street hack? By God, if that's your game!

— Nothing of the kind. Let me reassure you, Mr Betty. I'm not interested in rattling any skeletons hidden in closets.

— If your mind is tending on those lines you can leave this house immediately.

— On my oath I do assure you. When our conversation has ended I shall leave this room and will never make further reference to you in print or speech. You have a fascinating history, Mr Betty, but that is what it is, history. I'm not a historian, I'm a writer. I'll not trouble you further after today but I would, for my own satisfaction, merely like to clear up a few loose ends that I found when writing out your story.

— I am not sure whether I like you, Mr Dickens. I thought I did but I find your manner somewhat impertinent.

— I'm sorry to hear that.

— Yes. You see, I do not care to have my word questioned. It makes me uneasy. I do not mind speaking of myself. I am used to that. I am also well-used to people writing about me — as you will know from the thousands of words in my cuttings book. But I detect a wariness in you. A suspicious nature that has something of the lawyer. And we all know what they are like!

— Indeed we do, as at one time I had aspirations to be one.

1827

His awful experiences of labouring at the blacking factory now well behind him but always to loom ominously in his memory, Charles had thought he might like to make a career in the law. The friend of a friend of his mother had managed to secure him a position at Ellis and Blackmore, a modest firm of solicitors. This was a position as a lowly clerk and paid a mere ten shillings and sixpence a week but the future prospects dangling tantalisingly before him made him feel that there were possibilities to achieve great things. Unfortunately he was not an articled clerk but, nevertheless, it was the first step on a possible ladder to fame and fortune and Charles strode off with a manly swagger. He was wearing a very smart new blue jacket with a military-style cap jauntily angled on the side of his head.

On his way down Chancery Lane he passed a rough labouring fellow who snapped to attention saluting derisorily.

"Aye-aye, captain! Ain't we the mighty soldier," said the ruffian with a fatuous smirk.

"Did you speak, fellow?" demanded Charles haughtily.

"Cor, d'ye think y'are the Duke of blooming Wellington?" laughed the man.

At that Charles punched the man on the nose. This was a mistake as he found out when the ruffian knocked his cap off and blacked his eye, and was only prevented from doing further mischief by Charles hastily running away.

Although the work was dull, principally involving copying and fetching and carrying documents between various public offices, Charles found his companions congenial, while they enjoyed his excellent mimicry of characters that abounded in the locality of the office. He was generally recognised as a smart young fellow and he certainly tried to maintain a fashionable appearance on his modest salary, that being gradually increased to fifteen shillings.

However, he soon realised that this work was only going to lead to a lifetime of drudgery. He would always be in an inferior position as his articled-clerk contemporaries progressed upwards in a proper career. Charles wanted to make his mark. He did not really care in what manner. He wanted fame for fame's sake. He wanted the name of Charles Dickens to resound through the metropolis so that no man, no matter how lowly, would have to ask "Who?"

— Now I think my opinion of lawyers coincides with yours, Mr Betty. You have nothing to fear, I assure you. As I say, I merely want to clear up a few aberrations to my own satisfaction. I think you will agree that, when you dictated your memoirs, I pointed out that I reserved the right to ask for elaboration on certain matters.

— Yes, and I reserve the right not to accede to your requests. Here, sir, take a glass. It is an excellent wine. It may make you less austere.

— Thank you.

— I usually take the odd glass of wine in the afternoon. My doctor says a bottle of wine a day is an excellent tonic. I am not sure about the ale at lunchtime and the spirits in the evening though, eh?

— One point on which you may be able to satisfy me is this. You said you came from a family of independent means and that you, yourself, were insistent about going on the stage.

— That is correct. After I saw Mrs Siddons act I declared that I would die if I could not be a player.

— So you enjoyed appearing as an actor?

— Immensely. It was my whole reason for living.

— If you were acting for pleasure and not for gain I would have thought that you would have confined your appearances. Perhaps a couple of times per week to indulge your pleasure. Your tours sound as joyous as a treadmill.

— But I was in demand. I was a Child of Nature. It was incumbent upon me to show my talents to as many people as possible. They used to actually fight to get in to see me. At Stockport where I was asked to do an extra performance, the only way to fit it in was to travel overnight and sleep on the coach, as I was due at Leicester the next evening. That's how in demand I was. They actually rang the church bells to announce the news we had agreed to an extra night. Of course they increased the admission charges for it.

— No doubt your Friends made these arrangements?

— Oh, yes, they saw to all that. I was the star. I left all the arrangements to them.

— I wonder if you recall an actress called Mrs Sinclair?

— No, should I? I worked with so many players. Hundreds of them. Poor drudges. I do not remember any of them except the well-known ones – Kemble, Cooke, Bannister – but these names will mean nothing to you, they are long gone. You can hardly expect me to remember every impoverished actor in every tin-pot company.

— I had a very interesting conversation with Mrs Sinclair. She said that when you came off the stage at the end of the performance you were quite exhausted. You were almost totally devoid of sensation. You had to be sustained with a mixture of rum and milk. You were fed daily with tonic pills to maintain your vitality, strength and stamina.

— Oh, yes, that is correct. I gave my all for my public. You see I was not a naturally strong boy. It was often remarked how such overwhelming power could issue from so frail a vessel.

— But surely a caring father would have been concerned at making his son's exertions so tortuous?

— What could we do? The people wanted me. They clamoured for me.

— But your health? You told me how you became gravely ill. I confess at the time I thought you perhaps exaggerated the public's interest. But I saw from the cuttings how it truly was of national concern. In fact your father was actually accused in the public press of exploiting you for gain.

— Some persons of a philanthropic but interfering disposition did cause a few comments to be printed. The sort of people who agitate about boys sent up to sweep chimneys, and children working in the mines. I was hardly in the same class as a sweep's boy. Those people should have stuck to what they know. From what you say it seems they would have been wiser to visit Warren's Blacking factory.

— Mrs Sinclair says –

— "Mrs Sinclair says" – are you going to take heed of the ancient gossip of a failed actress who probably never earned more than ten shillings a week in her entire life? I could command fifty pounds a night. A night! This is all before your time, Dickens. I do not know how you have the gall to offer up these criticisms. The biggest star in the theatrical firmament was Kemble and he had a salary of thirty-seven pounds ten shillings a week. A week. And he engaged me for twelve nights at fifty guineas a night. So do not tell me about players. Nobody – nobody – earned the money I earned in one year. Not even David Garrick himself came anywhere near to it.

— I do understand. This confirms that your father's object was to make as much money out of you as humanly possible.

— If you were paid fifty pounds for writing a newspaper article and were told you could have fifty pounds a time for as many articles as you could write, would you confine yourself to one article a week? Of course not. You would be scribbling non-stop from dawn to dusk. And overnight too I'll be bound.

— But that would be my choice. No one could compel me now, only my own ambition or greed. Your father was responsible for what you were obliged to do, just as my parents condemned me.

— Well *my* father was a wonderful man. Wonderful. He was full of gaiety and joy. We were a very united and happy family. Oh, I will agree that he occasionally lost money on a few of his ventures but he always came up smiling. Everybody liked my father. He was a hearty man. Always popular, always the centre of a crowd in the saloon or in the market place. I am not going to sit here and let you denigrate my father. He loved me and he loved my mother. He promised her that she should never want and, when things were not going well for the family, somehow he always pulled us out of the mire.

— By exploiting his son.

— Exploit, exploit. For God's sake man. Talk sense. You were in a blacking factory at twelve years old and you talk about exploit! I was earning fifty pounds a night, not a shilling a day! I was mixing with nobility. I dined with princes. The Prince of Wales wished to oversee my education. Lord Eldon offered to put me under the protection of the Chancery Court. Do you think these great men would have suffered any exploitation of me? I was dressed in the finest raiment. I was painted by the most eminent artists. I was privileged. Do you not realise that I was one of the richest persons in the kingdom in 1805? You talk twaddle.

— It merely struck me that, as a delicate boy, your health should have been of concern.

— It was of concern. It concerned the entire nation. When I was taken ill they had to cancel all my engagements. My life was despaired of. When the news was announced all London sent to enquire. The Prince of Wales himself sent his own doctors to see me.

— I have now seen one of the Northcote engravings. I agree you were a fine-looking boy.

— My father commissioned that. It was very popular in its day. It sold several thousand copies at half-a-guinea a time.

— It does seem to me that your father never missed an opportunity to pull his family "out of the mire".

— He made a solemn promise to my mother. We had been forced to leave our house in Ireland —

— You lost that too?

— Yes, yes. But what of it? My father made it all back.

— I rather think Master Betty made the money back.

— My father recognised I had been blessed with particular gifts. He was always afraid they might desert me. The gifts coming from God rested on a purity and innocence that would not last for ever. My voice would break. My beautiful looks may desert me with increasing age. As indeed they have. Even I, looking in the glass, cannot pretend I see any sign of lingering beauty there. If I complained about the work all this was patiently explained to me.

— So you did sometimes complain?

— Yes, of course. I was a boy. I wanted to do boyish things but I seldom could. I was always rehearsing, travelling or playing. Playing on the stage when I wanted to play in the fields with ball or kite.

— I hesitate to quote Mrs Sinclair again, but she recollects an incident when you were informed in the green-room that you were to perform for the following two nights and you replied "They may as well kill me now".

— I was an actor. As a child I was given to dramatic statements off the stage too.

— But you did not protest in earnest? You did not ever refuse to do as you were bid?

— I do not know how it is today, Mr Dickens, but in those days children obeyed their parents. It was our duty to do as we were told. Our parents knew what was best for us and we obeyed them.

— You said that your mother was not in favour of your proceedings – she called it vagabondage.

— Look around you, sir. This is a fine house is it not? I have a cottage in the country where my mother still resides in peace and plenty. When my father died he left fifty thousand pounds to me. That is what my vagabondage brought. I live free from want, free from care. That is entirely due to my father husbanding his wealth. That was the sort of man he was. So disabuse yourself of any thoughts that I bear any resentment towards him. I loved my father. He was a wonderful man. Wonderful.

— I'm sure he was.

— I remember once that he got a very good offer for me to appear at the theatre in Lewes. That is near the coast of Sussex. We could have done it easily. It was when I had two days free during my Drury Lane contract. We could have travelled down by coach one day, performed that night and returned the next day. But my father would not contemplate it. No, he said, those two days were for resting in.

— Very wise.

— There you are. When the papers complained about his overworking me he printed that story. So that showed them. Anyway we were invited to Carlton House that night. The Prince of Wales used to throw the most splendid soirées. The best parties I ever attended.

— Although, I understand that when Drury Lane was closed for Passion Week, your father tried to engage you to a theatre in Coventry.

— That is correct but I did not do it.

— No?

— No; we went all the way up there, then at the last minute the theatre was not allowed to open. The Bishop or somebody complained. All theatres closed for Passion Week in those days.

— I fear I have trespassed too much on your time already but may I raise one final point before I go?

— Am I able to prevent you?

— When you dictated your memoirs to me you never mentioned William Hough.

— Why should I?

— Wasn't he your dramatic tutor?

— I did not need a dramatic tutor. My gifts were God-given. That was the whole point. That was why I was a phenomenon. I was a prodigy. God chooses a certain child and blesses him with extraordinary powers that are not given to ordinary men.

— So if Hough was not your dramatic tutor, who was he?

— Mr Hough? Just a man that my father employed.

— I've seen a print depicting a Mr William Hough described as Dramatic Tutor to the Young Roscius.

— No doubt he ordered the picture done and described himself thus for his own vanity.

— So in what position was he employed by your father?

— Oh, very menial. Arranging the transportation, hotels and so forth. A lackey.

— My acquaintance Mrs Sinclair tells me that when you were first introduced into the company assembled in the green-room you were accompanied by Mr Hough. He was your dramatic tutor and was at all the rehearsals and, in fact, trained you in your parts.

— I have told you not to rely too much on Mrs Sinclair's word.

— I think you will like what she wrote to me recently in answer to a query I made. I asked for her impressions on first seeing the Young Roscius. May I read this to you?

— Can I stop you?

— "Master Betty was a complete vision of beauty. He bowed in an elegant manner as Mr M'Cready the theatre manager introduced him and his tutor to the company. The latter kept aloof as the boy went round the room and shook hands with all in a free and winning manner devoid of either bashfulness or boldness. He played Norval and his youthful figure was graceful in the extreme and the picturesque Highland costume displayed it to the utmost advantage. His features were delicate but somewhat feminine; his eyes were a full bright and shining blue; his fair hair was long and hung in ringlets over his shoulders. In the daytime rehearsals these abundant tresses were confined in a comb which, still more, gave the idea of a female in male costume."

— That is how I was at the time.

— Didn't you resent appearing effeminate?

— You are impertinent, Mr Dickens.

— Some unkind reports say you had a feminine appearance to go with your feminine name.

— I am not so unworldly that I do not know that for every person who offers praise there are two to censure and slander. Malicious paragraphs were printed. It is the lot of any man, or boy, who is an outstanding success, to cause envy in lesser persons. My parents were always proud of my golden ringlets. I know a few derogatory remarks were passed but many more extolled that same appearance. The *Ladies Magazine* said that "female beauty cannot afford anything more sweet than his smile and the whole Town is in love with him." Something like that.

— I've read many such passages.

— Fashions change. Do I appear effeminate now?

— Not in the least I assure you.

— If I, in my turn, may be impertinent I would remark that you, yourself, Mr Dickens, appear to be inordinately proud of your locks.

— Mrs Sinclair goes on to say "I saw one of his marked sides, with lines for the proper inflection of the voice, and instructions as to action: here raise your voice – lower your voice here – put the right leg forward here – withdraw it here!"

— What of that?

— Is that usual?

— Sides are an actor's part written out. He does not have the full text of the play. Just his own role. He is quite at liberty to mark his sides in any way he chooses to assist himself while preparing a part.

— So it is customary?

— Quite usual.

— But in your case your part was marked up by Mr Hough so that you knew how to say your words and how to carry out your actions.

— All that is nothing. That is the workaday task of any actor. What counts is the performance on the stage. I, sir, was a God-given genius; I did not require instruction. I had no need of artifice.

— So Mr Hough was not your dramatic tutor?

— I would prefer you not to proceed with your questions regarding Mr Hough.

— I'm sorry if I've caused offence.

— I am not offended. I simply do not wish to search my brain to recall every Tom, Dick & Harry who thought it was a privilege to scrape acquaintance with Young Roscius.

— I'm sorry. I had the impression that Mr Hough was very important in your career.

— No.

— In fact I was under the impression that the term 'Master Betty's Friends' referred to your father and Mr Hough jointly.

— Stop talking about Mr Hough! I do not want to hear his name again!

— Mrs Sinclair was very young at the time, perhaps her recollections play her false.

— I have done my best to forget Mr Hough. I do not thank you for raising old ghosts.

— Then let us talk of something else. What was your favourite role?

— We discussed that at length on your previous visit.

— So we did. Young Norval. Mr Home the author of the play said you played the part exactly as he'd envisaged it. I believe you said your mother is still alive?

— Yes. Yes she is.

— Do you see much of her?

— Indeed I visit her quite regularly. She lives very near to where I was born. She never comes to London. Her age and state of health preclude that.

— No doubt you sit and chat about the old days.

— No. She did not approve of the 'old days' as you call them. I thought I had made that sufficiently clear.

— Of course – vagabondage. After your triumphant London season you said your father obtained greatly enhanced terms for your return the following year.

— He was very astute.

MAY 1805

The London season came to its appointed end. Covent Garden closed with *Othello* – Mr Kemble as the Moor, Mr Cooke as Iago. In these two equal roles the play was more like a gladiatorial combat as the old protagonists tried to upstage each other for the greater glory of the drama. At the end of the evening, in a transport of enthusiasm caused by the triumphant delineations, some wag called out "No more Boy's Play!" – a cry which was taken up by others.

Mrs Siddons, who had declined to appear at all during Master Betty's seasons, did not take to the stage again until later in the year when she undertook some limited engagements in several provincial cities.

Back in December, when the Betty entourage had arrived in London, Mr Betty was not to know that both theatres were then in a parlous financial position. He did not realise that it was this desperate situation that had enabled him to do the deal with both houses. Both managers knew that whichever theatre failed to capture Master Betty would soon go under. In six months Young Roscius had added forty thousand pounds to Drury Lane's balance sheet and staved off bankruptcy. Covent Garden had been in little better state and Young Roscius indeed had proved to be the saviour of both theatres. As a result Mr Sheridan and Mr Harris were resigned to not having the exclusive services of the marvellous boy and, being so grateful to him, it was rumoured that his father was able to extort a hundred pounds a night from them for the following season.

John Philip Kemble was in a very invidious position at Covent Garden since, as well as being its star actor, he was also the manager holding a sixth of the equity. As a player, indeed the acknowledged head of the profession, he deeply resented having to give way to what he considered the amateur antics of a schoolboy and thought it outrageous that he should have to pay the father vast sums of money for his services but, as a manager, he knew he had to put on what the public demanded. Kemble would prefer that his theatre staged the finest serious drama every night but he knew there was a limited audience for that and so must also give them operas, pantomimes and lighter fare.

Thus Kemble was obliged to follow Mr Harris's instructions and re-engage the prodigy for the 1805/06 season.

— More triumphs in your second season, Mr Betty?

— Yes, Mr Dickens, more triumphs!

— I believe that the fashion for Master Betty had somewhat waned.

— Is that what you believe, Dickens?

— Is that not so?

— It was the death of Nelson that made them stay away. The whole country was in mourning. Our political leaders were dead, the enemy was at the gates. Buonaparte was poised to sweep into our nation at any moment. People could not be expected to delight in the theatre in such times. All right. No doubt you have been prying into your newspaper archives and know what really happened.

The fashion, as you call it, had not waned – it had been deliberately killed, Dickens. I could still have pulled them in. I did – the season started wonderfully. I took three hundred and nine pounds at my benefit. All right, I admit that was somewhat down on the previous year but not to be sneezed at! I still had my following. But jealous actors purposely thwarted me.

— In what way?

— In every way. Bloody actors!

— But surely they were your own companions?

— Companions! Acting is a competitive business, Dickens. We are all up there trying to win the public's favour. At the end of the play each player wants it to be himself who is called for. Nobody else. Me, me; a player's life is all me – me – me!

— So what did these actors do?

— They set out to destroy me.

— Destroy you?

— Yes. Malevolently and deliberately.

— How?

— Ridicule. They tried to ridicule me. They placed malicious statements in the papers. They said my father had refused my services to play at a benefit night for the Old Actors Theatrical Fund. It was said that I was the only actor who had ever refused to play for the Fund.

— And was it true? Had he refused?

— I don't know! I was only a boy! I had no say in all that! Nothing of that was to do with me.

MAY 1805

As Young Roscius' exultant season was approaching its end his services were requested for one of the highlights of the theatrical season – the annual performance for the Royal Theatrical Fund, a charity which supported old and impoverished actors. On this one night of the year actors from both theatres were permitted to act together in scenes, or give soliloquies, in a gala night at inflated prices to swell the funds of this worthwhile charity which supported the old indigent players who had provided so much entertainment over the years.

There was a special interest this particular year as a supplicant for aid was the widow of Charles Macklin. Macklin had been very famous in his day on several accounts. He had been the first actor to play Shylock as a tragic, rather than a comic, character; he had killed a fellow actor in a quarrel over a wig but, most notably, he had not retired from the stage until the age of ninety-two when his memory failed him. He had died in 1797 aged ninety-seven, leaving a much younger wife and very little money.

Master Betty, if asked, would have liked to have helped Macklin's widow because he had heard many stories of the man from Mr Cooke who knew and idolised him. Cooke was recognised as Macklin's natural successor, taking over the comic parts of Sir Archy MacSarcasm and Sir Pertinax MacSychophant that the old had written and played so successfully. But Master Betty knew nothing of the attempts to succour the indigent widow.

Mr Moody, who was in charge of the proceedings that year, approached Mr Betty by letter, well in advance, to obtain the services of his son. Mr Betty, however, who was having such a jolly social time that he did not fully attend to his son's business apart from making astute contracts for inflated fees, neglected to reply to the letter. Six weeks later a personal approach was made by Mr Moody who was kept waiting for a full hour before Mr Betty deigned to see him.

"So good of you to see me, Mr Betty," said Moody politely.

"Come to the point, sir. I am a busy man," replied Betty brusquely.

"As are we all, sir, trying to get the Theatrical Fund Evening arranged."

"Well, what do you want?"

"We were hoping to hear from you about the appearance of your son during the evening."

"What evening? I don't know what you are talking about."

"Mr Maddox the secretary wrote to you some weeks ago about the matter. Next week is the annual charity performance for the Royal Theatrical Fund."

"Oh, is it? So?"

"It is considered an honour to be invited to take part."

"What is the purpose?"

"To raise funds to alleviate the unfortunate and distressed members of the profession."

"I see. Those who cannot obtain a place are to rely on the successful players to keep them in a state of comfort and idleness. It would be more to the point if these distressed players took to the stage themselves. No, I cannot allow my son to take part. You must know that he recently suffered a calamitous illness himself and was unable to perform for an entire month. Did he receive aid from your Fund then? No. The doctors have insisted that Master Betty husbands his strength and plays no more than three times a week. I cannot allow him to risk breaking doctors' orders."

"But perhaps he could forego another of his appearances that week?"

"Nonsense, sir! Are you advocating breaking a legal contract with our managers? It were best Mr Sheridan and Mr Harris could not hear you. Enough! Away!"

When the performance duly took place without a contribution from Master Betty many eyebrows were raised and the story of the father's refusal began to circulate. At his next performance Master Betty was astonished to be greeted by some boos and catcalls mingled amongst his usual nightly entrance ovation. William, of course, had no knowledge of the reason.

That night in a letter to his sister Augusta, Lord George Byron exaggeratedly reported that he had seen Young Roscius several times but at the hazard of his life from the affectionate squeezes of the surrounding crowd. As might be expected from a sixteen-year-old youth with histrionic and literary ambitions, Byron, loftily condescending from his superior position in society, was far from impressed by Master Betty's performances.

— They even kicked up a fuss about my pictures at the Royal Academy.

— I don't understand.

— Well Opie and Northcote wanted to exhibit their pictures of me but my father objected. He had commissioned engravings and he had the sole selling rights. For some reason that antagonised people.

— Ah! But these things were the acts of your Friends. Surely your personal popularity with the public would not be affected?

— The public are notoriously fickle. Tell them that something is the height of fashion and they all clamour for it. Tell them something is passé, and nobody wants it. Perhaps you will have heard of the South Sea Bubble? No? The South Sea Bubble was a financial scandal a hundred years ago. Everybody wanted to buy shares in the South Sea Company and a buying frenzy arose. The price soared to astronomical heights before it crashed, ruining many people. Mania and frenzy. Entirely a thing of fashion with no substance. Everybody wanting what the other fellow has. There is a madness that seizes men in crowds. They do not behave like independent entities but like sheep; their individual brains and thoughts are over-ridden by a mass movement. I realise now that Master Betty was the thespian equivalent.

— You spoke of ridicule?

— Actors are jealous men. They do not like other people getting acclaim. On my first season in London John Philip Kemble and Mrs Siddons stayed off the boards all the time I was there. They did not refuse to work but simply declined to appear until I was well out of way. As they were at the head of the profession they were in a position to do that.

MAY 1805

Mrs Siddons and her niece were out shopping for material. They were especially keen to find something suitable for new dresses as the latest Paris fashions called for an appraisal of new colours and fabrics. Sarah Siddons was one of the most well-known names in London. All classes of people knew of her. Even people who had never entered a theatre in their lives knew she was the leading player in all the country and had been so for over twenty years. While many of the more sober-minded people had a horror of the theatre and thought the inhabitants of that world were dissolute, dishonest and sexually promiscuous, even they respected Mrs Siddons as an exception. Mrs Siddons was not just at the head of her profession, she was a figure of moral authority, a person esteemed and admired by all.

Born into the long-established Kemble theatrical family, one of eight surviving children who all entered the theatrical profession – her brothers included John Philip, Charles, Roger and Stephen Kemble – she had known no other life. She had married an actor called William Siddons who was nothing more elevated than the son of an inn-keeper in Walsall. But despite all these handicaps to respectability Mrs Siddons had, through her work and her demeanour, ascended to her present lofty height where no one man or woman had a wrong word to say about her. Though not universally loved, she was admired and respected by all. Neither had she succeeded through her looks – she was no stunning beauty; while being slim of figure and attractive enough of face in her youth, these were never outstanding assets. She had not lost any of her following as she had aged and her slim figure thickened.

Of course Mrs Siddons was not a perfect woman, much less

faultless. Neither were people unaware of those faults. Neither was her life and career free from scandal and gossip, yet she rose above it all. By her exceptional stage presence, her commanding manner, an aura of personal dignity, integrity and moral authority she overcame all. As an actress she had exceptional assets in her voice, face, eyes, body and bearing which she controlled with consummate artistry and skill. After years of tramping the provinces she made an appearance in London in 1782 at the age of twenty-seven and became overnight, beyond all comparison, the leading tragedienne of the English stage. She was not a naturally humorous woman but, while never acceptable in comedy, in tragedy she had the ability to make the very angels weep.

Mrs Siddons claimed that she now only performed for the money to keep her children fed, clothed and respectable. In 1784 she said her ambition was to make ten thousand pounds so she could retire. She had achieved that by 1786. Now secure in her position she curtailed her appearances, only acting some fifty times a year but, as she commanded fifty pounds a time, she was content. However, unknown to her public, her apparently charmed life was beset with repeated illnesses: piles, rheumatism, chronic headaches, disease of the mouth; while Mr Siddons was rumoured to have passed on the clap to her. As a result of these trials she was addicted to laudanum. There was also the necessity to support her aged parents, unsuccessful husband, her seven children and assist her many siblings. Quite recently she had suffered the loss of two of her daughters: Sally aged twenty-eight and Maria aged nineteen.

Although entitled to large salaries she was often unpaid and, over the years, Sheridan himself was indebted to her for several thousands of pounds. Every year she threatened retirement saying she was only going on to support her family. Fortunately she had now amicably separated from Mr Siddons who had the knack of letting his wife's money dribble away in ill-conceived ventures. Because of his ill-health it was decided that he should dwell in Bath, settle twenty thousand pounds on his wife immediately and leave the other twenty thousand pounds of the estate to his wife on his death. A not unreasonable arrangement considering that she had earned all that, and more, in the first place.

Although England had a Queen and a Princess of Wales, as far as the general public was concerned they were minor royalty compared to the Queen of Tragedy.

Mrs Siddons suggested that her niece hold up various fancy ribbons against the material they were currently considering but her niece, not being a professional juggler, was in difficulty holding the several spools as well as the heavy bolt of cloth.

"Give me the braid!" declaimed Mrs Siddons. Two ladies in a distant part of the shop exchanged knowing glances. They could not see the owner of the voice but they had often heard much the same delivery in a line about daggers in the play *Macbeth*.

"Will it wash?" The tones were not dissimilar to the blood-curdling lines of tragedy with which she regularly wrung the withers of the theatre-going populace. The draper hurriedly assured her that it would. Mrs Siddons, of course, believed him because her habitual air of uncompromising principle compelled honesty in others. The draper was a theatre-goer and worshipped Mrs Siddons and hardly dare venture to speak to the goddess but, plucking up his courage, he asked when she would tread the boards again because she had not been seen at all in the current season.

"I shall resume when that puppet has left! Have six yards of this bolt sent to my house," she replied grandly, and swept out of the shop.

— It was all right for stars like Kemble and Mrs Siddons to remain aloof and not deign to work. The other actors had to go on – they were not stars, they needed the money. They were ordered to support me, so had to do it. But they did not like it. None of them did.

— But Kemble was the manager of Covent Garden as well as its leading actor; surely he must have made a great deal of money from your seasons?

— Of course he did. But that was all that interested him. He had no choice. If I had been appearing exclusively at Drury Lane then not a soul would have gone to Covent Garden. Kemble was only the manager. He was under orders from Harris, the owner. He had to have me to compete with the other house. Politics, Dickens. I was an innocent lad. I was a pawn in all these machinations.

— You said that you were deliberately destroyed. What happened?

— Two weeks prior to my own second season Kemble himself engaged an infant phenomenon called Miss Mudie.

— Another phenomenon?

— After my success they sprang up all over – including Miss Mudie the Infant Roscia. Everybody was trying to ride my horse. On her first night they had the poor child playing Peggy in *The Country Girl*.

NOVEMBER 1805

"Come in Charles, have a seat. I just want to set out the pro-gramme for next week." John Philip Kemble waved his brother into his office. "Here is the list," said he, handing over a paper.

Charles Kemble glanced down it. "*The County Girl* again? We only did it last week. I did not think Miss Searle was greeted with much approbation otherwise I would have announced a repetition on the night."

"This will not be Miss Searle."

"Oh? Then who?"

"Miss Mudie."

"Who the devil's Miss Mudie? I hope you are not succumb-ing to promoting some doxy whom one of your friend's happens to admire."

"Really, Charles, how could you accuse your manager, much less your brother, of doing such a thing? I am a theatre manager not some sort of pander making gain out of pushing some harlot in front of the public. I know less reputable theatres take money from rich old men who wish to further the aims of their, er – "

"Mistresses?" offered Charles.

"I was going to say wards," replied John Philip loftily. "Anyway, Miss Mudie would be appalled to hear her acting manager describe her in such terms as you imply. She is very genteel."

"Oh, yes. Well where is she from? I have never seen any reports of her from other theatres."

"No, no. She is very new. Very. But I am assured that she is exceedingly talented and has played first-rate comic characters in Birmingham and Liverpool."

"Have you seen her? Auditioned her?"

"No, I have not auditioned her, but I have met the young lady. Her tutor brought her in."

"Tutor?"

"Yes."

"This sounds ominous, John. What have you done?"

"I have engaged Miss Mudie to perform the role of Peggy in *The Country Girl*. Mr Brunton as Belville, Mr Murray as the pretend husband. You, Charles, will give your Harcourt. 23rd November."

"What's this about her tutor?"

"She has a tutor to assist her with the roles."

"She's not one of these infant prodigies, is she? Since Master Betty they've sprung up all over the place. We've been offered Master Benwell from Chester, Miss Fisher from Bath, Master Brown the Ormskirk Roscius, Master Mori the Young Orpheus. Drury Lane has engaged a four-year-old trumpeter, for God's sake!"

"Please don't blaspheme, Charles."

"How old is this Miss Mudie?"

"I understand she is quite petite."

"Never mind the size. How old?"

"Eight."

"Eight?" cried Charles Kemble amazed. "Eight? Are you mad?"

"Not at all. The public seems to desire infants, so we shall provide them."

"After all you've said about Master Betty! I cannot believe this! Anyway Betty himself is due back in December."

"I am aware of that, Charles."

"This is ridiculous. Betty Senior will be furious, you realise that?"

"This establishment is not run for the purpose of keeping Mr Betty in a placid mood," replied John Philip loftily.

"You're doing this on purpose, aren't you, John?"

"I certainly don't engage performers by accident."

"You know what I mean; you know this will undermine

Young Roscius."

"Surely not. Master Betty is the superior of Garrick. It says so in all the newspapers."

"This is some devious ploy that you're cooking up."

"You do not usually challenge my authority, Charles."

"I am not challenging your authority now. I do, however, suspect an ulterior motive."

"Please arrange the printing – Miss Mudie, only eight years old, first appearance in London, hailed throughout the provinces for her remarkable comic ability, you know the usual sort of thing."

"Very good, John, it shall be done. Just remember I consider it most unwise and am totally opposed."

"Of course I shall remember, Charles, but I expect the evening will pass off exactly as planned."

It was an unusually small audience that gathered for Miss Mudie's debut. When Miss Mudie entered, not only did the audience see an eight-year-old child, they saw a particularly diminutive one with two absent front teeth. Her performance was received in good humour and the sight of Mr Murray, not a tall man, having to stoop to pat her head and bend double to kiss her, caused some chuckles. When Peggy had to pat her guardian's cheek Mr Murray was almost compelled to go on all fours. As the play progressed and Peggy was talked of in terms of a 'wife' and a 'mistress' a great amount of hissing and laughter arose. As Peggy became the cause of Belville's amour, and her guardian's despair of another man taking her, the audience found it too ludicrous to be endured any longer and started shouting "Off! Off!" The crowd became divided between those who laughed at the absurdity of it all and those who found the utterances of a grown man to a little girl in matters of love to be an obscenity.

To Charles Kemble's distress he was responsible for the final debacle when he had to utter the line "Let me introduce you, you should know each other, you are very like and of the same age." This was too much and the howls of derision brought the play to a halt.

With the tumult rapidly developing, the precocious Miss Mudie tried to calm things by stepping forward to say "Ladies and gentlemen, I have done nothing to offend you, and as for those who are sent here to hiss me, I will be much obliged to you to turn them out." This speech had the immediate effect of causing half the audience to cheer sarcastically whilst the other, taking extreme offence at being harangued by a tiny child, increased the clamour. As the determined child stood her ground Charles Kemble was forced to go on to try and calm matters.

"Will you permit Miss Mudie to finish the play?" he desperately supplicated.

In the tumult there was no doubt that the majority opinion could be succinctly rendered as "No! Off!" Bowing to the inevitable, as well as the audience, Mr Charles Kemble took the child's hand and led her from the stage. He returned to announce the play would resume very shortly with Miss Searle in the part of Peggy. The audience applauded, Kemble bowed and Miss Mudie disappeared into theatrical history.

After the performance Mr Charles Kemble wrote a report of the evening for his brother Mr John Philip Kemble and had it sent round to his house.

"Is anything the matter, dear?" asked Mrs Kemble when she saw her husband read the message just received.

"Oh, no, no. Nothing at all. The evening passed off much as expected."

— Miss Mudie's debacle became the talk of the town. But that was not the worst of it. It was the newspapers reporting on the event. They said they were tired of money-grabbing fathers who considered themselves more fortunate to have a spouting child than a five-legged sheep. Implying that I was no better than a freak! Money-getting managers ransacking day-schools for actors is an insult to the commonsense of the public. All that sort of thing. I will never forget the invective heaped on my head as a result of these other children. It was all planned to destroy me!

— All this immediately before your own season was due to start?

— Exactly. The whole thing was carefully planned by enemies. Poor Miss Mudie was put up simply to bring me down.

— It must have been horrible for both of you as you were mere children.

— Well, of course, that was another thing. I had grown in a year. I was taller, my voice had broken. My features were losing their refinement. The press seized on all these things to denigrate me. Newspapers print what is sent to them. A person with the proper skills can insinuate anything into the papers. They will print whatever suits them at the time. They can always retract and apologise if necessary after they have done their damage. The reader always believes the original statement, never the apology. The papers that had lauded me to the skies one year did their damnedest to tear me down the next.

— I'm afraid the British press takes delight in debasing the heroes it has itself built up. It doubles the sales. The editions sold praising a person can be reworked by inserting phrases like "This paper deplores" and "It is shame on the nation that" in front of exactly the same material and then sold again.

DECEMBER 1805

Mr Edward Bishop and Mr Anthony Johnson were close friends of long standing. It was their custom to meet up virtually every weekday at the Piazza Coffee House to catch up on the gossip of the Town and read the papers. They were such old friends that some days they barely spoke to each other at all but chatted to many of their mutual and separate acquaintances. While both were absorbed in reading different newspapers, Mr Bishop remarked "I see your hero's back."

"Why do you say my hero? Surely he is the nation's hero? Your hero, everyone's hero? Do you not admire our late Admiral Nelson?" replied Mr Johnson.

"I was not referring to that gallant and lamented man. I mean the actor – Betty. Young Roscius returns tonight."

"Oh, I see. Of course I am aware of his return but I do not know why you refer to him in that foolish way. To call him my hero!" said Mr Johnson hotly.

"Well, Anthony, you did drag me with you to see all his appearances last season, and you did express the opinion that you had never previously seen his like."

"Yes, I did see Master Betty play all his roles. I did not drag you along, you were most eager to accompany me. All the Town flocked to see him, as you well know. It is foolish to call him my hero."

"Well, in addition to seeing him in all his roles, I seem to remember your going from stationer to stationer looking for prints of him. You bought pictures of him as Selim, Hamlet, Frederick, Norval – "

"There's no need to go on," said Mr Johnson huffily.

"Then there was that day I had to accompany you as you searched everywhere for a picture of him as Osman," chaffed Mr Bishop.

"I don't see anything wrong in trying to assemble a complete collection of an actor's roles. Why do you think they publish them? Lots of people collect pictures of players they admire. And not just players. Don't tell me you do not possess a portrait of Lord Nelson?"

"Well yes I do," confessed Mr Bishop.

"There you are then," said Mr Johnson with satisfaction, as though some legal point had been proved.

"There's no need to be so touchy, Anthony. I was only saying that the boy is back."

"Yes, well, I know you do not regard the theatre as important as I do, but I do not like to hear you mock my passion."

"And is your passion the theatre or Master Betty?" provoked Mr Bishop with a smirk.

"Do not presume on our friendship too much, Edward. If you do not withdraw that remark I shall have to call you outside," said Mr Johnson rising threateningly to his feet.

"Oh, don't be so sensitive, Anthony. 'Tis merely a tease. You must not rise to my bait so readily."

"Yes, well, I don't think it very amusing," replied Mr Johnson sulkily slumping on his chair.

Mr Bishop, liking his friend very much and knowing his personality inside out, always knew when to withdraw the needle before any serious breach and he deftly moved the topic sideways. "I see that Mr Betty Senior has posted a notice in all the papers about the fact he would not permit the boy to appear for the Theatrical Fund last May."

He held out the newspaper for his companion to read.

'Manchester, 2nd December 1805

Sir,

Having read a public letter respecting my having refused to let my son perform for the Theatrical

Funds, I take leave to make a few comments thereon. Although the engagements I was under rendered it impossible, without incurring a heavy penalty, for my son to play last season, it was well-known it was his wish, and my full intention, he should perform for that excellent institution. If the reports, circulated with so much industry, have been kept up with a view to irritate, and induce me to refuse my assent to my son's performing for the charity alluded to, until some apology be made for such malignant aspersions, the author will be disappointed of his aim. The best answer to such attempts to degrade me, and injure my son in the estimation of the public, is to take this method of declaring, that my son will perform for the joint benefit of the decayed actors at Drury-lane and Covent-garden, any night the committee appointed for each fund shall, in conjunction with the managers of either theatre they may wish him to perform at.

I am, Sir, your very humble servant,
W. H. Betty'

"Stupid man. He alienates everybody with his high-handed manner. Then when the public shows its displeasure the poor lad has to bear the brunt."

"I would have thought it rather late in the day for issuing an apology. On the one hand he claims that he was restricted by positive engagements and heavy penalties, now the gossip is that he says that he did it on doctors' advice; that he did not want to over-tax his son after his illness. He says his son is now in excellent health and he offers his services gratis for any similar event this season."

"Of course you know why he has apologised? Do you not find it significant that this apology, which should have been made months ago, now arrives just two weeks after that horrid little Mudie child was booed off the stage?" said Mr Johnson with a meaningful look.

"Ah, I see. Fear is the spur."

"It is true I admire Young Roscius. I think he is a very talented boy, but his father is a monster. They say he has extorted a hundred pounds a night out of Harris and Sheridan for his son's appearances this season. And he never misses an opportunity to boost the boy and screw more money in whatever way he can. Did you know he is proposing that a statue be erected by public subscription?"

"The man is mad, is he drunk with power? Surely he must realise that, when Parliament is considering such measures to honour Lord Nelson, this proposal of his can only alienate the very public he is trying to woo?" asked Mr Bishop.

"How can one nation produce a man like Nelson then on the other hand a scoundrel like Betty?" wondered Mr Johnson.

"Betty is Irish of course," conceded Mr Bishop.

"That's true," agreed Mr Johnson, as though the fact put a whole new understandable light on the matter.

"Lord Nelson's body has arrived at Spithead. It has taken a long time," said Mr Bishop, thinking it diplomatic not to delve further into the monstrous Mr Betty's affairs in case he set his friend off again.

One of Mr Johnson's traits was his assumption that nobody else knew what he knew even though he had gained his knowledge via the public press. "It has taken five weeks to bring it from Gibraltar. The seas have been so rough. They took Nelson's body there after the battle. It took them seven days to do that because HMS Victory was so badly damaged."

"I understand the body was placed in a cask of brandy to preserve it," added Mr Bishop.

"Indeed, that was the only thing to hand whilst out at sea."

"Would rum not have been plentiful? Surely rum would have been better anyway?"

"No, no. Brandy is far superior to rum for preservation purposes. Of course spirit of wine is best of all but they could not get that until they reached Gibraltar."

"And is it true that on the long journey they had to keep topping up the cask?"

"Oh, yes. To keep the liquid fresh they draw it off at the bottom and replenish from the top."

"I believe that the sailors drank the spirit drawn off," said Mr Bishop.

"How disgusting! Where on earth did you hear that?" asked Mr Johnson.

"I thought it was common knowledge."

"I've not heard that," protested Mr Johnson.

"Oh, well, if *you've* not heard, who knows of the truth of it?"

"Surely even seamen are not so desperate for liquor?"

"No, no – you misunderstand. They wished to imbibe the Nelson spirit. They wanted to have a part of the great hero inside them. No man has ever captured the adoration of his men like Nelson."

"No man has ever done so much for his country," said Mr Johnson shaking his head.

"That's true. There will be a state funeral of course."

"Of course. The nation is in mourning, we must have an opportunity to display our grief."

"We look to our players to lift our hearts in these doleful times. What's Master Betty playing tonight, Anthony?"

"Young Norval in *Douglas*."

"No doubt you will be there?"

"Most certainly. Do you wish to accompany me?"

"Why not?" answered Mr Bishop, gesturing to the waiter.

— In spite of the viciousness of the press and alienated employees I had a successful season. I even performed on the evening of Nelson's funeral. We all went to watch Lord Nelson's funeral procession. It was a solemn affair but such a historic moment that although Marianne was only a baby my father told my mother to bring her too so, when grown into an old lady, she could say that she had seen Nelson's funeral. Alas she was not destined to grow into an old lady. We watched the solemn parade from Whitehall where Father had obtained very good seats in a stand. It took fully four hours to pass by because there were so many marching. Father said the only navy people in the procession were Greenwich pensioners and Nelson's officers, with some members of the crew. I think this was because the entire navy would have wanted to be in the procession and, as that was not possible, these were the privileged group. There were thousands of spectators; I had never before seen so many people in one place. The carriage that bore Nelson's corpse was decorated like his ship with all the hero's battle honours hanging for everyone to see.

At night I had to play Norval at Covent Garden. Cooke was Glenalvon and he had been drinking again which made him imperfect in his words. He said he had been toasting the fallen hero. At one point in the play no cues were forthcoming. He had no idea where he was. Then he marched forward and said "Ladies and Gentlemen, as there is no accounting for the timidity of young actors, especially before such a distinguished audience, this young gentleman will, I hope, experience that lenity you have so often showed on similar occasions. His fears have caused some little inaccuracy, which I trust will not be repeated." He then made his bow and walked off. He left me there, stranded, as though it had been my fault. Mr Charles Kemble, who was in the wings, gave him his words and pushed Cooke back on. He was able to take up his lines but I do not know whether the audience realised it was his fault and not mine.

In all the parts I have played I have never once had to rely on the prompter. I did not lose money for the managers either and that is all they cared about. In my entire life I have never lost money for the management. But I cannot deny that, as you say, I was out of fashion. My appearances were reduced to one a week. People had seen me in the same parts before anyway.

— Could you not get up new ones?

— Yes. I essayed one or two. I played Richard III again. But it was not the same. Kind people said I had grown and was more manly. But I was not manly enough to be a regular actor and I was past being an infant prodigy. I attempted Macbeth, acquitting myself most honourably in the part, but there was a lot of dissent. In fact quite a disputation arose between my followers and my detractors about my ability in the role.

JANUARY 1806

On the 5th January Young Roscius made his debut as Macbeth. He had been urged to play the role while he was in Scotland but, instead, Mr Jackson had commissioned a new play expressly to show off his talents. A local author, who had never written a play before, came up with a tragedy called *Henry of Transtamare* and Master Betty had been obliged to play that instead. It was fustian rubbish and William, knowing his father would not want him to play it again, promptly wiped the lines from his mind.

While his audiences wanted to see Young Roscius in the roles he was famous for, there was a limit to the number of times he could repeat these favourites and still expect to fill theatres. Because of his excellent memory he was able to undertake new roles at short notice and his plays roamed widely through the current repertory, occasionally alighting on a part that he could, and did, add to his stock of personal favourites. However, to take on a part such as Macbeth was to flirt with the image of actors who had made the part very much their own. The memory of Garrick was still vivid in the minds of older playgoers, and Kemble was the man of the moment.

Since his return the London public realised that this was a rather different Master Betty from the one who had left them only a few months before. In his absence his voice had broken and he had grown considerably. Not only upwards but outwards too. Young Roscius was in danger of becoming chubby. The pale, frail vessel now came before them as a well-fed hearty. As usual, opinions were divided, some saying that he had lost his looks, others saying he was now more 'manly'. Some regretted the loss of sweetness in his voice, others called it a harsh rasp, others said he projected it far more effectively into the vast reaches of the auditorium. In the event the evening could be called a draw, the members of the audience being pretty evenly split 50/50 in their opinion.

In the first light of day a huddle of soldiers from the nearby barracks grouped in St James's Park. Early morning mist hovered over the lake and the air was chill. Captain Poulter and Captain Bryce had come to fight a duel. Although duels were strictly forbidden by both army and government, men of honour still resorted to this practice of settling disputes.

The two captains were colleagues and were accompanied by their friends. The previous evening they had been a merry party, dining and wining and attending the theatre in Covent Garden. It was hard to believe that these were the same gentlemen who had laughed and roistered a mere few hours previously. They had already agreed that the weapons should be pistols so there was little ceremony to precede the action. Neither of the combatants now really wanted to proceed with the duel. In the cold, sober light of day both men realised they had been ridiculous the night before but neither knew the other's innermost thoughts. The trouble with many young men, especially the sort who become soldiers and excel at their profession, is that they are able to convince others by an outward show of bravery. They are able to suppress their private thoughts and lead their colleagues into all kinds of danger. If such young men thought more, and longer, rather than acting swiftly and briefly, much less harm would be done in the world.

So the duelling procedure continued with a minimum of speech until one of the company could contain himself no longer. "Stop this, you fellows! This is nonsense! What are you arguing about? A mere pomping boy!"

For the cause of the duel was none other than Master Betty the Young Roscius who, at that moment, curled up in a deep sleep in his bed, was oblivious to the very existence of gallant soldiers named Poulter and Bryce. The group of friends had been to see Master Betty give his Macbeth, after which Captain Bryce stated his opinion that he had "Never been more vastly entertained by any player he had ever seen. The boy was a heaven-sent genius and could act any adult player off the stage." This opinion, widely held by many people and given extensive dissemination in the public press, offended Captain Poulter who stoutly maintained that the stellar attraction was "No more than a personable youth of ordinary accomplishments who had a retentive memory and a pleasant but thin voice. Any schoolboy of good education could do the same." Because the colleagues had been drinking, these two opposed opinions were inflated into a matter of great importance. What was merely a difference of opinion became a heated argument, developed into a matter of personal insult, and led eventually to a challenge and a duel.

The sensible friend went on "So one of you thinks the lad is a genius, the other says he is commonplace. So what? One of you likes custard pies, the other doesn't. You, Jim, like the skirl of the bagpipes – you, Ted, can't abide the very sound! Do you argue about that? No! Of course not. It's personal choice. The same with this player. Some like him, some don't. I personally can't abide Mrs Siddons but thousands admire her – so what? See some sense you fellows and drop this at once." The other soldiers murmured assent because, whilst last night they took sides and egged the captains on, now they realised that if they persisted in this folly the result could be the death of one of their friends. "Nobody will think any the worse of either of you. It was the drink talking last night. Come on, shake hands. Forget the player. Put him with the bagpipes and the custard pies; really to you he is nothing more."

Fortunately Captain Bryce and Captain Poulter saw the sense in the words of their colleague and, handing back the duelling pistols to the referee, embraced each other warmly for they had always been good friends since joining the army.

And the custard pie slumbered on oblivious to the trouble he had so innocently caused.

— But you said when dictating your memoirs that though your second season was blighted by world events it was by no means the end of your career as Young Roscius.

— Most certainly not! I returned to the provinces. I had a reputation that still counted for something. Of course many big theatres taking their lead from London were closed to us but we soldiered on. We played anywhere that would pay the money. I could still command anything between fifty and a hundred pounds a week, plus a benefit, at some country theatre. You see, all over the land there were people who had heard of Master Betty, read of Master Betty and wanted to see the wonderful boy for themselves. So, to satisfy this demand, we were able to tour for years.

OCTOBER 1806

Stephen Kemble, brother of John Philip Kemble and Mrs Siddons, had made a special visit to London to engage the young actor who was the talk of the country. After seeing Master Betty in action he wrote to his wife that, although the whole business with the boy was a humbug, he had engaged him for their theatre in Newcastle.

Mr Liston the well-known comic actor was a close friend of Mr and Mrs Stephen Kemble so, some time later when the bills went up announcing the appearance of Master Betty, he called in one morning to see Kemble and found him pouring over the advanced bookings list.

"Good morning to you, Mr Kemble, you look very satisfied with yourself if I may venture so."

"Indeed, Mr Liston, I am perusing the box-list for the Betty engagement."

"Do you consider the engagement will turn out well?" asked Liston.

"It cannot be otherwise, sir, with his stupendous abilities," said Kemble, regarding Liston in a manner that suggested he was foolish to even doubt it.

"You astound me, sir. I was not aware you held such a high opinion of the boy."

"Sir," replied Kemble emphatically, "I look upon Master Betty to be a great – nay, the greatest tragic performer that has ever appeared on these or any other boards!"

"I presume you except Mrs Siddons and Mr John Philip Kemble," protested Liston.

"Sir, I except nobody. I maintain that Master Betty is the finest actor now living, and could well be the finest actor who ever lived!"

"But I must press you, sir. Mrs Kemble confided in me that in the letter you sent to her from London you expressed a rather different opinion. How do you reconcile this current high praise with that?"

"Ah, since my first opinion I have engaged him, sir!" and Kemble, leaning back, guffawed so much that his Falstaffian body shook with hearty appreciation of his own wit.

— You still attracted good audiences in the provinces then? No doubt people came through curiosity.

— I prefer to think of it as by reputation. They came to see me so that they could tell their grandchildren they had seen the wonderful Master Betty. People now say I was a nine days' wonder. But I had a very full and exhausting five years on the stage. By the age of seventeen I had done and seen more than most men manage in a lifetime. I knew all the nobility, I had dined at their houses. Unless I gambled it away I had more money than I could spend should I live to be ninety. Not many men can retire with a large fortune at the age of seventeen.

— What made you return to the stage after your father died?

— Boredom.

— You missed the acclaim of the crowds?

— I still had a love for the profession. After all, a great part of my short life had been devoted to it. I looked at it this way. I still had my reputation and I was now a grown man. I was twenty years old. I had learned a great deal. I had learned all about the art of acting and the ways of the theatre. I reckoned that if I were good as a boy, think how much superior I would be as a man. So I decided to return to the stage. I embarked on my second career as an actor. I was on my own this time.

— No father and Friends to control and comfort you.

— That is so.

— But your reputation still lived. You still commanded a large salary.

— Indeed I did. I made several provincial engagements to get back into the way of things, then once again made my assault upon the capital.

— And were you acclaimed?

— I was engaged for twelve nights before Christmas and twelve nights after Christmas, at my old money – fifty guineas a night with a clear benefit.

— But were you acclaimed? I believe some of the London newspapers were somewhat – er, unmoved?

— They were scathing! They slaughtered me! Bastards the lot of them! *The Times* especially. They listed all the attributes necessary to be an actor and ended up by saying I was deficient in all of them. They came every time I played and always slandered me afterwards. They said they could not understand how, in former times, the great and good had been betrayed into their absurdities. One of their reports actually said "it would serve no purpose to reveal how often this commonplace player left your reporter in irresistible slumber." Boasting that the hack slept through my performance!

— It seems to me that, in some measure, you were being blamed as a man for the folly of the public idolising you as a boy.

— That is it! You have hit it exactly, sir! They seemed ashamed that they had ever acknowledged my genius.

— No doubt the public had a sense of guilt for behaving in such a frenzied hysterical manner. Your return gave them a golden opportunity to atone for their previous aberration. *You* were made to suffer for *their* folly.

— They said I was no good. I tried new parts. I starred in *Alexander the Great*. Some said my voice was harsh, some said I spoke as though I were at the tea table, others said I ranted. In other words I could please no one. It was a stupid play anyway.

— Did you complete your season?

— Of course. I have never lost money for any management. Although the twenty-four nights ended up being spread over five months. But I had many old friends in the provinces. On hearing of my return, old Mr M'Cready at Newcastle immediately asked for my available dates.

— Was his son treading the boards by that time?

1812

At the Theatre Royal Newcastle the forty-seven-year-old Mrs Sarah Siddons was in the midst of her farewell tour. She had just departed from the stage after playing Mrs Beverley in *The Gamester*. Her leading man for the occasion, playing the role of her husband Mr Beverley, was the nineteen-year-old William Charles Macready. No one seemed to think the discrepancy of age between Mr and Mrs Beverley at all odd. It was accepted that the local leading man would play the lead, be it Romeo or Lear, and the visiting star whatever their age would play the star part, even if it be Juliet. Before leaving the theatre Mrs Siddons sent for her erstwhile stage husband.

"You are in the right way," she told him, "but remember what I say to you now: study, study, study, and do not marry until you are thirty. I rather think a certain lady of your company may have designs on you. You are not an unattractive young man so I warn you to beware."

Macready stammered that he had no such distractions and that he was dedicated to his work.

"When I was a young woman starting out in this profession I was hampered by a husband and small children. They were a constant impediment to the smooth furtherance of my practice."

Macready, already a serious man, who thought Mrs Siddons the nearest thing to perfection in her art, resolved to heed her words.

William M'Cready – the boy whose father had so assiduously kept him from being contaminated by the stage, who was to be an educated gentleman, the youth who was to train for the law – was obliged to leave school at the age of sixteen with no thought of university or any further education. M'Cready Senior had entered into a speculative venture constructing a new theatre in Manchester. This had turned out to be a disaster as it coincided with a depression in all classes of industry and a sixty per cent increase in the price of wheat. In a matter of weeks M'Cready was heavily in debt and in November 1809 made bankrupt. His son William, a serious and worldly youth, devoted all his efforts to saving his father from debtors' prison. In that he failed as M'Cready was imprisoned for some months but, by taking over his father's company, he managed to turn things around and slowly began to clear debts and obtain his father's release.

By June 1810 William M'Cready had re-invented himself as William Charles Macready the eminent tragedian. He had made his debut as Romeo and, seeing no viable alternative, reluctantly started his career as an actor.

— Oh, yes, my old play fellow had made his debut during my recess. He was very much the coming man when I returned to the stage. We acted a great deal together. I can tell you that William Macready had a very good opinion of me. Many a night I acted him off the stage. Have you been to see this new Yankee tragedian? Forrest. I went to see him the other night. He is deliberately throwing down the gauntlet to Macready. Challenging him in all his favourite parts. Macready will hate that. He is a very vain-glorious man. He loathes competition. Forrest is excellent even if he is a Yankee. It is time Macready was taken down a peg or two. He has lorded it up too long. I should think he is damned grateful that I am retired.

— I hear that Macready assaulted the manager of Drury Lane.

— Bunn is a philistine. He cares nothing for art. But he insulted Macready once too often. Bunn tried to keep him in thrall by every means he could. He deliberately announced that stupid evening comprising the first three acts of *Richard III*; *The Jewess* — nothing but a tawdry spectacle; and the first act of *Chevy Chase*. A ridiculous programme. It was a calculated insult, of course; Macready's finest effects are in Acts IV and V of *Richard*. Macready was outraged but had he refused to play he would have broken his contract and lost two hundred and fifty pounds. Neither would he want to put his future reliability in jeopardy. The word would soon get round to other managers. He begrudgingly went along with this ludicrous proposal. I am told that he gave a very poor showing because of his mortification and, coming offstage in a fit of temper, roared "You damned scoundrel! How dare you use me in this manner!" and attacked Bunn. I believe there was some feeble grappling and the combatants were easily pulled apart by arrivals who had heard the fracas.

He was dismissed, of course, but he would have walked out anyway. Now Bunn is taking him to court for common assault. I do not know what the theatre world is coming to.

— I've heard persistent rumours that Macready is going to take over

Covent Garden.

— God, I hope not. He is insufferable enough as it is!

— He will restore its reputation as a temple of the drama.

— Aye, a temple with him as its tin-pot god.

— It's strange how things fall out, isn't it? You were both talented young actors, yet you retired while he now heads the profession. You have no regrets about retiring when you did?

— Not for an instant. I am well out of the hurly-burly. It is not as it was. There are no true artistes any more. The theatre is run by business men nowadays. Philistines like Bunn. All they care about is profit. I see you look at your watch. Pray do not let me keep you from the charms of Miss Burdett Coutts.

— Tell me about Mr Hough.

— There is nothing to tell.

— He seems to have been a remarkable fellow. In spite of your denials I know you owe everything to Mr Hough. Your father wasn't versed in the ways of the stage. It was Hough who was entirely responsible. He was the prompter at the Belfast theatre. He took you up as a boy right at the very beginning. Trained you to act. Obtained your first engagements in Ireland. Hough had many colleagues he could approach. Your father didn't know any theatrical people at that time. Hough convinced managers to engage you. Hough wrote all the newspaper puffs extolling your many virtues. Ingratiated himself with editors so that they'd print anything he told them. He built you up into the height of fashion. He put you in a position whereby you could earn fifty pounds a night. And all that he did for fifty shillings a week.

— Four pounds ten shillings plus his keep.

— A remarkable man and so self-effacing. He stayed in the background so you could have all the glory. But, as your success grew, your father became more confident. He started asking for sums of money far beyond Hough's experience. Hough would never have engaged you to both houses at the same time. He knew that was not done. But then, at your very pinnacle of fame, there was a disagreement between Mr Hough and your father. It was a very quarrelsome falling-out. A public squabble in the daily press. I have copies of some of the statements here. "This suspension of Friendship does not arise from any avariciousness on the part of Mr Hough who discovered, cultivated and anxiously advanced the

Interest of the *fortunate* family, without any real regard for that of his own. No, his affectionate attachment to the *extraordinary boy* was far paramount to any pecuniary or personal considerations. He was only actuated by professional pride, laudable ambition and the most sincere regard for the fortune and fame of his adopted Theatrical Child."

— As you said, Mr Hough had insinuated himself very well with the gentlemen of the press.

— *The Sun* said "As the Boy's *very wonderful* success is generally understood to have been the result of Mr Hough's unremitting tuition, it is to be hoped that Mr Hough is permitted to have some share of the *golden harvest* upon principles of gratitude as well as *justice*." It would seem Mr Hough felt that he should have some reward greater than four pounds ten shillings a week plus his keep. Is that what your Friends fell out about? Money?

— Mr Hough had the press in his pocket; he could tell them anything. He bribed them. My father provided him with the money. Money that I earned. Then Mr Hough used our own money to turn the press against us.

— Why should he do that? He placed advertisements in all the newspapers. He proclaimed he would publish an appeal to the British Public. "Hough versus Betty Senior in which William Hough the late dramatic tutor to the Young Roscius would reveal a curious correspondence, with explanatory notes, concerning the career of Master Betty. He would trust to the candour and judgment of an impartial British Public." What did your Friends fall out about?

— Were you not able to find out? You do surprise me, Dickens. You have revealed yourself to be a consummate delver into the darker recesses of the human soul.

— I found no record of anything after his advertisements. William Hough seems to have vanished from the pages of the public press. What happened when he published his appeal?

— He never did publish it.

— Why not?

— Because he would have had to reveal too much about himself. My father arranged he should have an annuity of fifty pounds a year and Mr Hough silently removed himself from our lives.

— A modest enough reward. Or was the annuity a form of blackmail?

Paying off a villain?

— Mr Hough was one of the kindest men in the world. He heard me recite at one of my mother's parties. He thought I had great promise and agreed to train me for the stage. He came to live with us. Mr Hough taught me how to deliver lines, how to carry myself, all about the techniques of stagecraft. He chose my parts, my plays. He arranged my debut. As you surmised, he saw to all the puffing in the press. Mr Hough obtained my first engagements. Yet he insisted that my father should sign the contracts. Mr Hough was naturally retiring and insisted that he should remain unknown. He was always solicitous about my welfare. He was horrified when my father started booking me for more than three nights in the week. He totally disapproved of my going to parties after the play and thoroughly blamed my father for forcing me to socialise with the gentry which was much against my will. Mr Hough was a kind and gentle man. When I was taken ill he blamed himself for not standing up to my father. He thought that between them they might have killed me.

— I've read comments about how your father was only interested in getting as many eggs as possible from his golden goose.

— Malicious but true. He screwed more money from the managers than Mr Hough could have imagined in his wildest dreams. Time and again Mr Hough tried to stand up for me against my father, but Dad always won. I cannot deny that Mr Hough was kinder, more concerned, more considerate than my own father. He cared for me. But he was weak and ineffectual. Time and time again he allowed my father to ride roughshod over him. I was a dutiful son and Dad took cruel advantage of that. He drove me very hard. It was all sport for him. He revelled in all the hysteria and agitation. I was terrified most of the time. Because he enjoyed roistering far into the night he did not realise the incessant travelling and public display was unsuitable for a frail young lad. Each night I flogged myself half-dead acting before the public. Even in the dressing-room afterwards I was on display – my very exhaustion a sport for spectators. A privilege to see my suffering. It may not be work like in a mine or a factory but, I tell you, it was still devilishly hard graft for a young 'un.

— If Hough was unable to stand up to your father, surely your mother – did she not protest?

— Dad was not a bad man; he was a loving husband and everybody liked him and he was great company, but he was full of blarney and bluster. He thought he was always right. That is why over the years he lost so much money. He gambled on fruitless ventures. He lost all my mother's estate, then his own. Half the money I made he lost with gambling and treating everybody all the time. He thought I was a never-ending flow of wealth. He worked me so hard because he needed the money. He needed it because at heart he was a wastrel. Thank God he died when he did and there was still a lot of money left – fifty thousand pounds. If he had lived longer he would have got through the lot. As it is he left me well provided for, so I have to thank him for that.

— Your father placed upon you responsibilities and cares that no parent should visit upon a son. To me he seems harsh and heartless. Pitiless and inhuman. Yet you honour his memory. Of Mr Hough, who did so much for you, who cared for you, who was kind and gentle, you will say nothing. Why?

You remain silent.

Why?

— Because he used me as his woman!

— I'm sorry. It was stupid of me to raise the matter.

— You stirred memories that quite unmanned me.

— I'm truly sorry.

— I thought I had forgotten. But one never forgets. Perhaps we should face up to our ghosts. My father should have known that a man who creates five hundred pounds a week for others will not be content with four pounds ten shillings as his portion. Unless there are other compensations. My father eventually realised, but not soon enough. Well, to finish the story. The 'true story' as you like to call it.

— Please. I would not cause you further distress for the world. I should go.

— Sit down, Dickens. The damage is done. And Miss Burdett Coutts can serve dinner without you. You are a spying, prying, conniving person. I dislike you intensely. Without Mr Hough I had only my father to rely on. Mother was too weak to stand up to him. We carried on and we did not miss Mr Hough one bit. We did not need him any more. I did not need to learn new roles. The business was rolling along. We did not have to do anything but turn up at the theatres and leave with sacks of gold. Then I grew up. That was all it was. I grew up. My father became less domineering simply because I was better able to stand up to him. I was bigger and stronger. We gave up because I was strong enough to say I did not want to do it any more. In any case by that time the work was diminishing. I went to university to please my mother. After my father died I tried to come back as an adult actor. In spite of what I told you to say in my memoir, I have to face up to the fact that, as a proper actor, I was not a success. In fact I was a dismal failure. My engagements started rapidly dwindling. I tried to take on new roles but somehow they never suited. I was forced to keep repeating my old parts. The gaps between engagements were getting longer and at the same time my remuneration was diminishing. I was grubbing about for five pounds a night. I did not need the money. I had plenty. But I needed to be a star. I had no Friends to tell me what to do. Mr Hough had gone, my father had gone. I was alone.

— No man needs to be a star.

— Perhaps not. But I did need to be an actor. When I was a child I said I would die if I could not be a player. Now I was a man I felt the same way.

— They say you cut your throat and were in mortal danger.

— I cut my throat and made a botch of it. I was in no danger. I could not even do that properly.

— But what caused you to make such a drastic attempt on your life?

— I had at long last managed to wangle another contract out of Covent Garden. It was my big chance again after so long in the darkness. Not at fifty guineas a night. Nothing like that. But a London appearance. They cancelled it. I was in despair. I was stupid. I thought it was important.

— Your family and friends must have been grateful for your ineptitude with the razor.

— Friends! What friends? I was an embarrassment to everybody. I was a ghost from history. I was foolish to go on. I had no need of the money. I was far wealthier than most actors can ever be. But money is not every-thing. I suppose I was still stage-struck. I needed to be a star. I thought I would make one last grand attempt to achieve popularity. Remind people that I was still alive and available for engagements. I threw a great dinner party. I invited all the leading men in the profession – Elliston, Matthews, Winston, actors, managers, prompters, playwrights, the lot. Even Macready who had done me much injury. I had to rent an auction room to accommodate all the guests. I invited all theatreland. Only eleven people turned up.

— I don't know what to say.

— I was a bore, Dickens. I had taken to drink. I was forever collaring people and telling them I used to be the famous Master Betty. People started avoiding me. Oh, I had plenty of larks with a few close friends. Mainly useless young fellows like myself. They got drunk on my money. Such larks we had! I tried to be happy but William Macready had blighted my life.

— Macready? In what way?

— I worked with William a lot after I came back. We were quite pals for a time. One day he let slip that my father knew what Mr Hough was doing to me long before the row when he got the sack.

— But that's abhorrent! It can't possibly be true!

— Of course I did not believe it. I do not believe it now. It was probably just malicious green-room gossip. But the seed of doubt had been planted. Once something has been said it can never be unsaid.

— What a wicked and cruel thing to say to a friend.

— He ceased to be a friend.

— I'm not surprised you cut him after that.

— On the contrary, it was Macready who dropped me. William did not want to be tainted by failure. As I sank, he rose upwards. I was in despair. I attempted to kill myself again. Not with the razor this time.

— I'm listening.

— One night in a drunken fit I tried to throw myself out of the window. I had chambers in Duke Street. Up two flights. I smashed through the window but got stuck on the sash. Already getting a bit portly. Two Bow Street officers were in the pub opposite and ran up and saved me. So I was cheated of death a second time.

— That I didn't know.

— It never made the papers. By that time my thwarted suicide was not even newsworthy.

— But your wife and son. Did you not consider them?

— No I did not. I was stupid and selfish. I thought I should be in the same position as William Macready. I had been a star at thirteen before he had even set a foot upon the stage. There I was, useless and forgotten at only thirty-three years of age. My old playmate Macready was being hailed as the successor to Kemble and was rapidly taking his place at the head of the profession. A position in which he is unrivalled to this day.

— It's clear you suffered much misfortune but many a man would envy you. You had a wife and child, a mother alive, property in Town and in the country. Ample money. Surely a man of strong character should have been able to put such adversity behind him.

— Well now, Dickens. It is odd that you should say that because one day I woke up. I do not know why, but I suddenly realised all those things you have just said. You are right. I was wallowing in self-pity. I was eating an apple at the time and I realised that my life had been just like an apple.

— An apple?

— Yes. When you eat an apple that first glorious crisp bite is heaven. A crispy, crunchy mouthful of goodness. That was me in my early Master Betty days. Then you take smaller bites and, yes, the apple still tastes good but you are becoming used to the flavour by now and it is tasting more commonplace. That was after my first manic season. Then you reach the core and you are nibbling about trying to get some decent nourishment from the hard unpleasant centre. That was how I was then. Nibbling for bits of glory. I realised I was foolish. I decided the thing was to put it all behind me. So I did. I formally announced my retirement and I have been a happy man ever since. The way to happiness is to look forward not back. It is perfectly possible to start eating another apple. That was twelve years ago and I have been contented and happy ever since. I do not envy any man.

— I wish I'd known all this when I wrote up your memoirs.

— Good God, man! Do you think I want all this revealing to the world? I am speaking to you in confidence. You promised not a word said would leave this room.

— I feel guilty that I did not hear your story with more sympathy.

— I do not need your sympathy, Mr Dickens. I asked you to write my official memoirs and you did so admirably. You carried out my wishes. Thoroughly and exactly. I could not have asked for a better job. Now when my son takes up the stage at the age of eighteen I will have those memoirs available for sale in all the theatres he plays.

— I thought your son was reluctant to take up the stage? Studying divinity.

— He will tread the boards. He will be the famous son of a famous father. Henry will not struggle as a common player. Through retirement I have ceased to be a humiliating failure but become well-respected. I am no longer in woeful competition. I am that grand old actor, the former Master Betty, known throughout the profession. I am on the free list at Drury Lane and Covent Garden. I have many friends and companions. I hob-nob in green-rooms and quaff Burton-ale in the bar. You see I am no longer an embarrassment. I am history. A history that is long ago. I am ranked with Trafalgar and the days of glory. I am thought of as a contemporary of Kemble and Kean, both dead. Yet I am only forty-six years old. Is not that odd? So my son will have much assistance when he takes up the stage as his career. He will not start out like Kean, a mountebank who languished for years in some tatty company playing Harlequin and Hamlet for a pound a week. No, sir. Henry will be a star. I will see to that. My son will strike Macready from his pomping pedestal. I will ensure that he knows all the parts, all the business that goes with them, all the points to be made, how all the speeches must be spoken. I still have my old sides all marked up.

— By Mr Hough?

— By Mr Hough. I shall be both father and dramatic tutor. Henry will be my new apple.

— Did you ever hear any more of Mr Hough?

— The last I heard was years ago – he was in Leeds with a Master Wilson, known as the Barnsley Roscius. I understand the boy had a squint, an impediment in his speech as well as an accent you could cut with a blunt knife. I can only assume he had an accommodating arse.

Mr Betty starts laughing; a grisly, appalling laugh that elides into an uncontrollable weeping. Dickens rises to his feet, looks on helplessly, stands hesitantly for a moment then picks up his hat, cane and cloak from the table, quietly lets himself out of the house and in the cold evening air swirls his beautiful new cloak around him and briskly sets off to a dinner engagement with Miss Burdett Coutts, the richest heiress in the country.

HISTORICAL NOTE

Master Betty and Charles Dickens were, of course, real people respectively aged forty-five and twenty-four in 1835. However, it is very unlikely that they ever actually met. The facts of Master Betty's phenomenal career and the persons connected with it – his father, Mr Hough, Kemble, Macready Snr and Jnr etc – are all accurate but I have interpreted the known facts imaginatively. In his Diaries William Charles Macready spoke kindly and highly of Betty and his abilities and there is no reason to suppose any animosity existed between them. Master Betty's son, known as Henry West Betty, made his professional debut at the age of eighteen at Hereford on 29th August 1838. Although his first London engagement was not until December 1844, Henry Betty soon established himself as a visiting star playing regular seasons at theatres such as the Theatre Royal Margate in 1839, 1840, 1842, 1846, 1847, 1848 and 1849 during which time Dickens must have seen him as he frequented that theatre on annual holidays. In 1854 at the age of thirty-five Henry Betty withdrew from the stage "to care for his ailing Father" apparently at his father's request. Master Betty died on 24th August 1874 at the age of eighty-three.

www.ingramcontent.com/pod-product-compliance
Lightning Source LLC
Chambersburg PA
CBHW030335180626
46810CB00003B/1369